. Meet Shadow, a beautiful Black Labrador/Greyhound mix, a dog with a sweet temperament and a need for speed. He has a few things to say...more than a few, actually. An entire year's worth! Welcome to...

The Shadow Diaries

In this heartfelt, funny, and ultimately inspiring memoir, Shadow recounts the first year that he came to live with his two Daddies, known as DJ and DS. Since they rescued him from the SPCA, Shadow chronicled his life in a weekly series of diary entries, first posted as a Facebook blog. From getting settled in his new home, to his Daddies learning his quirks (there are many!), to celebrations and holidays and road trips, Shadow experienced so much.

Now, all those of his adventures have been compiled together in this volume, representing a progression of three lives sharing their days, their nights, laughing and bonding with every passing season.

Along the way, Shadow shares stories of other dogs and how he met his extended family. He even sings songs! He narrates the story of a wedding. He learns about art and about theatre. But what he most likes are his daily walks. By day, he has lots of energy and loves to play "Triple Fetch." At night, though, he enjoys snouncing. It's a word he made up.

Filled with poignancy, humor, and heart, THE SHADOW DIARIES will restore your faith in all the good that exists in the world. Shadow's unique story is an expression of the joys we seek in our lives. This insightful pup reveals what we all know in our souls. Indeed, this Shadow knows the secret to life.

The final entry reveals Shadow's ultimate truth. But as he sings at one point, "Let's start at the very beginning." It's a very good place to start.

A dog can change your life. Your life can rescue his.

"Woof! Shadow is an inspiration to all canines and humans alike. His words make my Mom laugh and cry! He's innocent and honest, and his stories teach us all about love, acceptance, and living in the moment. Awesome read."

--Annie, Black Mouth Cur, Holden, MA

"With a name like Hamish, I find it ever so proper to support the able publication of *The Shadow Diaries*. Shadow is thoughtful and erudite, perhaps at times a tad silly. But he spins a good tale, all while twaping his own tail. He does enjoy word play, as do I. Cheers to the book!"

--Hamish, Lab Border Collie mix, Oneida, NY

THE *Shadow* DIARIES

The Hopeful Year of a Rescue Dog

Written by SHADOW
As told to Joseph Pittman

Published by
MLR Press, LLC
3052 Gaines Waterport Rd.
Albion, NY 14411

Visit ManLoveRomance Press, LLC on the Internet:
www.mlrpress.com

Original Cover Art by Steve Cummings
Editing and Interior Layout by Kris Jacen

Print ISBN #978-1-64122-316-4
ebook also available

Issued 2020

This book is dedicated to

DS, Misty and Bongo

"*The Shadow Diaries* holds a special place in my heart. Why? Because I got to write one! See, his two Daddies were visiting our house, while Shadow stayed at a doggie hotel. So I, along with Lucy and Marcy, took over for that week, and are now so excited to be part of the publication. Triple Woof to a dog who loves playing Triple Fetch."

--Gustavo (Gus), Golden Retriever, with an assist from Lucy and Marcy, Beagles, Syracuse, NY

"Shadow is one of my very best buddies, but who knew he was such an eloquent storyteller. His sensitive and heartfelt writing moves me to stop and pee on the roses."

--Ziggy, Welsh Corgi, Morris County, NJ

Author's Note

Hi Everyone, it's Shadow. Welcome to my year-long diary. These entries are unedited, which means they appear in this book as they did on my Facebook blog each and every week. For an entire year, I expressed my thoughts about my life and the world around me, about the experiences too of my two Daddies. Along the way, we became a family built on love.

I invite you to my story. It's unique, but it's universal.

You can also follow me on Instagram to see all the photographs that accompanied each diary. Find me at theshadowdiariesbook.

Thanks for reading.

"As two rescue dogs, we have loved our communications with Shadow! He is a bright, wildly articulate canine, and an amazing spokes-pup for us all. We have enjoyed Shadow's weekly diary. You, too, will fall in love with this prodigious pooch and his devoted Dads, just as we did."

--Mo, Bichon Mix, and Louie, Miniature Poodle, Long Island, NY

A Forever Home by *Joseph Pittman*

To get to know Shadow, I guess you need to get to know his parents first. I am a novelist, having published 13 novels under my name and nearly thirty under the name Adam Carpenter. Steve is my husband, my best friend, an elementary art teacher and artist whose work has been exhibited locally. We reside in a cute coastal village on the northern edge of the Jersey Shore. I also work what we call "front of house" on Broadway in New York City. But those are jobs. Our life is here, along a picturesque, windswept bay.

What we both wanted was to enhance our life with a....dog. Boy, did we luck out.

Okay, now that you know a bit about us, and you'll learn more through the course of the diaries, let's learn how we became a family.

See, Shadow almost didn't happen! At least, for us.

It was December 28, 2018, three days after Christmas and just a horrible day outside. Torrential rain drowning the Jersey Shore. Steve was off from school that entire holiday week, and I was home all day before my evening shift in the city. We'd made plans for that day but the weather was putting a literal damper on them.

Our original idea was to drive down to the SPCA in Eatontown, about fifteen minutes down the Garden State Parkway from our home in Keyport. We'd been talking about getting a dog together. When I met Steve in June of 2016, he had a

beautiful beagle-mix hound named Bongo, whom he'd rescued at the same location we were thinking of going to on this day. Sadly, Bongo passed in April of 2017. I'd only known him for nine months. He made quite an impression on me. At the time, I lived in Manhattan, but I welcomed coming to the Shore to see Bongo...um, I mean Steve.

It took a year and a half, but Steve was ready to start thinking about maybe possibly potentially getting a dog. Do you sense the hesitation there? Yeah, he loved the idea of a dog, but there was something about having a looser schedule. Not bound by meals, walking, peeing and pooping and playing fetch. Not being responsible for anyone other than himself, and me of course.

We'd gone to the SPCA a couple times over the past months, but we really never connected with the dogs we saw. I was close, once, a cute mix by the name of Max. He had a lot of energy, perhaps too much. But in the end, we left without a dog. But still thinking, eventually, it would happen.

It happened so quickly on that day!

With the rain pelting the land, Steve and I looked at each other and said, "well, we'll go another day." But then, it was almost like another force was in control, because the heavens closed, the rain stopped for a while. Maybe even the sun came out, though that could also just be fantasy. In any event, we decided to venture out and do as we'd planned.

Lunch first, a visit to Barnes & Noble. We're book and movie people. Not unusual for us. But then...we drove to the SPCA and went to look at two particular dogs we'd seen on their website. We saw them in their cages (I hate that word). While cute, their personalities just didn't connect with us. One even growled at us. I was beginning to think our visit was a bust.

And then.

And then... (yes, it bears repeating)

I turned around, and in his cage, behind plexiglass, was this skinny, gentle, adorable dog. I noticed the paperwork at the top of his door. His name: Shadow. He'd only been at the SPCA since December 20, 2018, just over a week. I bent down and met him eye to eye. Oh, the look I received back. It melted my heart. Then he reached out a paw and softly scratched the glass. As though he were saying hi. I said hi back, and then I said these fateful words:

"Steve, there's a black lab."

Shadow was pitch black, not a white hair on him unless you count his whiskers. What was also unusual was his sleek frame and very long legs. The nice folks at the SPCA had his weight at 18 pounds. He was one year and ten months, fully grown, healthy if maybe a bit malnourished. But those amber eyes. They didn't just look at you. They looked into you.

I knew I wanted to take this sweet baby with us and give him a home. I'm the impulsive one. Steve, on the other hand, and smartly so, did things properly.

First, Shadow was brought outdoors to the dog run, where we could watch him in action, just Steve, me, and the adoption counselor. And, well, of course Shadow. He was excited to get out of his cage. He ran around, happily, joyfully, expounding his energy and showing off his speed. If the fence hadn't kept him locked in, who knows how far he would have gone!

Then we went inside, to a meet and greet room. Quiet, still the four of us. The counselor handed us some treats, which Shadow accepted. Again, his approach was gentle. There was nothing aggressive about him. I remember looking over at Steve,

and I could see his heart was beginning to melt, too. Me, I was a puddle!

Shadow reminded me so much of Misty, the black lab who I grew up with. We got Misty when I was eight, had her until I was 22. So, I was familiar with the temperament of a black lab, and I knew, while they had some neurotic tendencies, the reward for having one in your life was indescribable. It was like Misty was letting me know I'd made the right choice.

As we played with Shadow in the enclosed room, I detected a couple looking in, almost...hovering. Shadow had more than one suitor! And the counselor said, "Hey Guys, if you're interested, I've got to tell you, I can't hold him. You have to make a decision." And then he put an explanation point on his words by saying, "Shadow is what we refer to as a highly adoptable dog." It was true, someone would adopt him today.

Quite frankly, I was surprised he lasted there eight days. Thank goodness for a busy holiday season.

We talked more with the counselor, we filled out paperwork. We picked out a red collar (in honor of Misty) and a purple harness (because it's Steve's favorite color). The SPCA did their due diligence, giving Shadow a quick physical, double-checking he was all in good health, his shots were given. Dotting the I's and crossing the T's. The nice couple who had been watching us watching Shadow came up to us and asked if we had adopted "that cute black lab." We did, we said. She seemed happy for us but disappointed. I understood. I would have felt the same. It had all come down to a matter of minutes.

And the next thing we knew, with the rain once again pouring down like cats and dogs (ha ha), the counselor brought Shadow outside to us. Steve unlocked the door of our SUV, got in the front. I hopped into the back seat, Shadow at my side.

This was real. He was coming home with us. As we pulled out of the parking lot, Shadow paced in the back seat, looking out the window, no doubt wondering what was going on and who were these two guys. His tongue, a menagerie of pink and black swirls, hung out. He panted. The rain continued to fall.

But he wasn't nervous. He wasn't scared. I think he was excited, and pleased to be away from that cage. It only took a few minutes and then he settled down, cuddling next to me as Steve drove toward home. I pet him, I kissed his head, I welcomed him to his new life. Time, though, was ticking away. It was after three o'clock in the afternoon and I had to catch a train. Steve might have been on vacation that week, but not me. I had a shift to work in the city.

Impulsively, crazily, happily, adopting a dog meant we were also unprepared for him at the house. Not like he was a baby we'd been expecting for nine months! First thing we did, stop at the grocery store. Our new boy needed food. Steve went shopping while I stayed with Shadow. We finally got home at 3:45, giving me only a half hour until my train. The last thing I wanted to do was leave! I mean, we'd just adopted him. What kind of Dad was I to leave fifteen minutes after bringing him to his forever home?

But first we had to get him into the house. He was hesitant, not because he didn't want to come inside, but because the floors prevented him from coming in. Our house has tiled floors on the back porch, up three stairs into the kitchen, which has the same flooring. Which to Shadow was...slippery. It took some coaxing, but finally he made his way up the stairs, into the kitchen, and to the carpeted dining room, living room and den. Shadow had begun to explore his new home.

And Steve and I had begun our new life, with what turned out to include a sweet natured, silly, fun, energetic puppy of a dog. Shadow had completed our little family.

That first weekend, as 2018 waned into a new year, I channeled my inner Shadow, and I wrote what would become his first diary entry—even though it didn't quite have a name yet. The Shadow Diaries wouldn't become formal until the fourth week. Once we had a title, I realized something special was happening. Every Sunday, I posted on Facebook the story of a dog. It was a hit! And now it's a book.

Shadow had a story to tell. Read on. It's fun and it's funny and it's sweet and its poignant, and ultimately, it's inspiring. A story of two men, one dog, and a year of adventures. Turn the page and go on an evolving series of stories that represent the life of a dog who defines love. From the initial tales of innocence to theme weeks and celebrations, a wedding, guest stars, road trips, The Shadow Diaries represents what can happen when you open your home, and your heart, to man's best friend.

Yes, we rescued him. But you know what, I think he rescued us.

THE *Shadow* DIARIES

"Listening to Mom read my Shadow's adventures was my favorite part of Sunday evenings after my walk. I don't usually get along with a lot of dogs. I like to think that everything around me is mine, but I would be willing to share my toys with Shadow. He's what people call a good dog He's smart, kind, and apparently loves playing catch. I hope that Shadow and I can play catch together sometime; maybe I'll even let him have the ball once or twice."

--Sadie "Monster", American Cocker Spaniel, Philadelphia, PA

Diary One

Hi Everyone! My name is Shadow. I'm almost 2 years old. They say I'm 48 pounds but some of that is holiday weight. My previous family couldn't keep me because of a bad man, a landlord was the word I heard.

Then, on December 20th I found myself living in a place where other dogs lived. Cats too, but...yuck. Anyway, I spent Christmas there, where nice people took care of me and gave me treats.

Then, yesterday, these two guys came to see me. They liked me enough to ask to play with me. We had fun. Then we went inside and had quiet time, and I decided I liked them. They both seemed to laugh when I licked their faces. Laughing is fun.

Long story short, I have a new home and from what Daddy Joe says, a really big family. Daddy Steve just said, "you have no idea". But you know, I'm warm and fed and happy and they had this toy for me to play with. They call him Bumble.

It's time for my first night here. I sure am comfortable except for the slippery floor in the kitchen. I'll have to work on that. Nothing is ever perfect, except this situation which has brought together three souls in search of family. I like that idea.

I also like that I'm the cutest of them all.

Hope to meet so many of you soon! I've already FaceTimed with 2 of my aunts. I'm thinking of getting my own Instagram account. For now, sleep time awaits.

Love, Shadow

Diary Two

Hi Everyone. It's Shadow, again. I'm just relaxing, as you can see.

I hijacked Daddy Joe's FB (I hear that's the lingo) again. And why not, he's not always around. He keeps saying he has to go to work with a monkey. Kong is his name. He might think he's a king but I'm a true prince and I can't wait to play with my two Daddies tonight. Even Daddy Joe said he'd stay home for a couple days. That will be fun.

I'm having a great time in my new home. The stairs still make me nervous but I'm trying. No, really, I am. Mostly. I like to play with toys and snuggling is the best. Walks are good too. Treats even better.

I even got to meet new people this weekend. I liked that! They were fun. But for now, it's soon time to play and then relax. Daddy Joe calls it his weekend. He sure has a weird schedule. But that's ok. Just know I'm happy. Daddy Steve has been taking really good care of me.

Love, Shadow

Diary Three

Hi Everyone. It's Shadow. Time for my weekly update.

Friday night was fun. Daddy Joe was home early (for him), so I got to nuzzle him while my legs were poised on Daddy Steve. I was right between them! I like that spot.

But I've really settled onto my spot in the living room, as you can see from my selfie. Plush sofa and pillows are very comfy. When I'm in my spot Daddy Joe calls me Sheldon. I thought my name was Shadow!

Also, Daddy Joe was under the weather Friday morning. I stayed with him for hours. I think he might like to snuggle more than me! That's really saying something! He's not a morning person. Neither am I, and I'm not even a person!

Daddy Steve likes to take pictures of me. He's also helped me get over my fear of those stairs in the kitchen. Sort of. They still freak me out. But I eventually go. Because I have to go outside and, well, go.

My home is warm and friendly and has yummy treats. I'm by myself right now but

I'm told Daddy Joe will be home first, soon. So I'm just gonna look out the window and wait.

Thanks for reading.

Love, Shadow Baby

"Hi, I'm Cooper, a four-year-old Lab, and I love when my Mommy and Daddy read *The Shadow Diaries* to me. I wish I could meet Shadow and show him my high desert home. We would have the best time but I'd have to teach him about cactus. Or, we could visit and run along the Jersey Shore. We don't have beaches here, so Shadow would have to show me the way."

--Cooper, Labrador, Sante Fe, NM

Diary Four

Hi Everyone, it's Shadow. Welcome to Volume 4 of what is now titled The Shadow Diaries.

So, it turns out that Daddy Joe (now DJ) writes books and they all have titles. So now my FB blog does too. He showed me the books but I just thought they were toys to chew. Good news is I ended up with a new nerf ball to chew nonstop. Yay!

It was an odd week. I wasn't at my best on Tuesday and Daddy Steve (now DS) and DJ we're worried about me. Such drama! I just needed some adjustment time. Turns out I have quite the independent streak.

But all is really good now. I love the walks in the neighborhood on my purple harness. I know I look good in my red collar but nothing like adding another splash of color! I've met neighbors and other dogs and construction workers!

I don't like when DJ leaves to see that monkey. That's when I try to eat his shoes to stop him from leaving. But he always comes back. Until then I watch movies with DS. Some of them are scary. That's why I cuddle with him.

Or I just go to my spot in the living room, where I strike a pose like the one below. Alexa, play Vogue! Okay, guess that's all I've got this week. Thanks for reading.

Love, Shadow Baby

"There's only one thing more exciting than the publication of *The Shadow Dairies*! It's playing with Shadow. I first met him at his house on July 4th, and boy, did we run and wrestle and have a blast. Then he came to visit me at my house on Christmas. We played some more and wrestled some more but during our quiet moments I got to tell him about our family's beloved Maggie. When I think of Shadow, I think of holidays and celebrations and how dogs bring us all together."

--Lily, Miniature Golden Doodle, Monroe, CT

Diary Five

Hi Everyone, it's Shadow. Time for my weekly update.

Actually I tried to post this earlier but FB wasn't working right. I lost all I wrote! Now I understand DJ's colorful language when he's at his computer.

Anyway, I've had a busy week. On Monday I had what's called a play date. I met Ivory, a really small Maltese doggie. We had fun even though she seemed scared. I'm bigger, yeah, but really friendly. thanks Danielle Perez and Todd Jackson for playing with me, too!

I went for walks every day, too. DS and DJ have different schedules, so I never know who will walk me. To my surprise, on Friday, they both did. I like when it's all three of us. Today I met more people. DS sure knows a lot of people! DJ finally came home after playing with his Kong. He thinks it's funny that my favorite toy is a Kong. I don't get it.

I also got new covers for the sofas. They are colorful and stylish, just like DS. Thanks for ordering them. That Amazon place sure has a lot of stuff for me. Wonder where their name came from. There's a lot to learn!

So, that's this week. Thanks for reading.

Love, Shadow Baby

Diary Six

Hi Everyone, it's Shadow. My weekly update is live.

First of all, thanks to all of you for reading. I love hearing your comments, which DJ and DS read to me. It's a big world out there, and it looks fun. When I'm not on my daily walk, I love to look out the window.

It was a quiet week. DJ was home days, and then DS most nights. I don't like Wednesday because I'm by myself a lot. DJ say he has to do a matinee. I don't like that word, but the way DJ says it I don't think he likes it either.

DS loves his nighttime snuggles with me. But I'll admit sometimes I need to run around and I do. Hey, I'm 2, it's what I do. But then I calm down and try and get the treat from my Kong. I take my time because I just like licking the peanut butter.

I love living here. DJ and DS do their own things sometimes and so that means I get to as well. DJ said it's called being independent together. DS laughed. He likes to laugh. Me, I just bark. And then we all cuddle on the bed and the world quiets down.

Well, that's all for now. Thanks for reading.

Love, Shadow Baby

Diary Seven

Hi Everyone, it's Shadow, it's that time again.

Seven weeks since I came to my forever home. Wow, to me that's like 49! Time sure flies when you're having fun. DS and DJ sure do love me. Always taking pictures and snuggling and giving me treats.

I've found a new spot in the afternoons. At the top of the stairs leading up to "the studio," as DJ calls it, there's a window which lets in lots of sunshine. I like the warmth, so I just hang out on the landing.

I continue to enjoy my walks and run around the yard playing ball. When I'm not outside I look out the front windows and watch all the activity. When the mail lady comes I kinda bark a lot. I'm just saying hi.

What I most like is seeing and hearing about other dogs. My little white doggie friend goes on walks too, and I bark hi at him all the time. I've also heard there's a new dog in the family, Lily. Yay! One day we'll meet and play.

I can tell DS and DJ are true dog people. In the kitchen are paintings of Bongo

and Misty (who I sort of resemble). I'm told they were really special. Lucky me that I get to follow in their pawsteps.

Well, I guess that's it for this week. Thanks for reading.

Love, Shadow Baby

"Shadow is not just a neighbor, he's our friend! He comes to our yard and we all run around and play. We all bark hello at each other on his walks. But then we found something out from our Moms—Shadow wrote a book! See, our paws barely reach the keyboard on the computer, so how he did it reminds us how long his legs are! His stories of life in our town remind us of the beauty and love that surround us all. Good job, Shadow!"

--Wally, Muppet/Mutt mix; and Bea, Meerkat/Mutt mix, Keyport, NJ

Diary Eight

Hi Everyone, it's Shadow. I've got words on my mind this week.

First of all, the word routine. I guess that's real life. DS goes to work during the day, DJ at night. One of them is usually home with me. We have a set pattern of who feeds, walks and plays with me.

Another word I learned is friendship. DS had people over on both Friday and Saturday. I got to say hi to new friends. Today I got to run around a backyard with two furry friends, Bea and Wally. They live close so we will play again.

The last word I discovered is a big one: Valentine. DJ gave DS a monkey on Thursday and they both laughed. I'm a dog. What's with this monkey DJ goes on about? Anyway, I got to pose in this photo with DS and the monkey.

DJ seemed happy to have his three Valentines in one photo. I like it too. But what I really learned is that all three words mean the same thing: I am loved.

Until next week.

Love, Shadow Baby

Diary Nine

Hi Everyone, Shadow here. Another week, another entry.

I wasn't sure what I would write about this week. It started out slow, kinda like me every morning. But as the days went by, activities became more rambunctious, kinda like me every night.

DS didn't feel good and stayed home from school. So I snuggled with him and tried to take away his misery. That's what I do. I give healing hugs. Today he's better. That makes me happy.

Last week DJ gave DS that monkey, but I couldn't play with him. This week my pal Ivory gave me a pig! I've already chewed off an ear. I think that's why I don't get the monkey. Thanks to Danielle Perez for my new toy.

Saturday night I was home but DJ was in "the city." He met a subway repairman (whatever that is) in front of his theatre. He claimed to be a sidewalk chalk artist on the side. See his handiwork in the photos. I like that I got to make my Broadway debut!

DJ told DS that story last night and laughed. As Cindy

Adams (whoever she is) says, "only in New York kids. Only in New York". Don't know why she has to say it twice.

Until next time. Thanks for reading.

Love, Shadow Baby

Diary Ten

Hi Everyone. It's Shadow. Let's see what's going on.

I want to discuss dogs. I'm one and in my neighborhood, there's a lot more! I'm always staring out the window hoping to see one. DS alluded to that in his post last night with that focused picture of me.

There's this fun white dog who I see every day on his walk. First I bark and then I wail because he's so cute and little and I want to play. Then I tear around the house, trying to see him from every window.

Then there are the dogs I meet on my walks. DJ and I met a new friend this week, a little pup named Rusty. He's much more fluffy than me. I saw him twice this week. I also said hi to my two friends Bea and Wally, and also to two big, fierce dogs who were thankfully in their yards.

But all this talk of dogs brings me back to where the week began. DS and DJ watched the Oscars (whatever those are) and I snuggled between them. DS wanted Roma to win. DJ guessed Green Book. I'm just glad Black Panther didn't win, because

panther is only another word for cat.

I'll stick with dogs.

Thanks for reading.

Love, Shadow Baby

Diary Eleven

Hi Everyone, yup it's me, Shadow. Has it already been another week?

A wise lady once said we will have weather, whether or not. DJ told me it was Grandma, Rosemary Pittman. I've got to say, she's right. Because this week we had it all.

Snow. I like snow. It's fluffy and I can bounce around in it, sniff it. I like when it tickles my nose. DJ made snowballs and threw them in the air and I tried to catch them before they went splat. Then I would try and eat them.

What I don't like is ice. The snow got hard and crunchy and took over my yard where I like to run. My paws don't like the texture. It kind of reminds me of the kitchen floor before we got those rugs.

But I think my least favorite is the rain. DS and DJ were going to treat me to a walk in town along the promenade. I know I would like to smell the ocean air. Instead, this morning it was raining cats and dogs. Not literally, that would look silly.

Anyway, that walk will have to wait. I just hung out in my spot, thinking about the lions and lambs of March, of Spring and of sunshine.

Thanks for reading.

Love, Shadow Baby

Diary Twelve

Hi Everyone, it's Shadow. This was a long week! I had that sense from the very start on Monday.

Speaking of senses, apparently dogs have higher senses than others. My sense of smell goes in overdrive on my daily walk. I sniff lawns and leaves and places other dogs have been. Then I let them know I've been there too.

My eyes work great, day or night. I can spot a cat or bird or squirrel like the hunting dog I am.

They cannot escape my sight. But on a leash I can't chase them. DS and DJ keep tight reins on me. But I see them...

I hear everything! A floor away, TV on, I can still detect the sound of a bag of snacks opening. Of course I go running up the stairs to try and get my share. Because...

My sense of taste knows no bounds. I like food. This Saturday I got breakfast and brunch because DJ and DS woke at different times. Yummy for me!

But the best sense is touch, because that's when I get to snuggle. Or just reach out one of my lanky paws to stretch and say hi. Whether it's watching a movie with DS or falling asleep next to DJ, I know I'm home.

But did you know there's a sixth sense? It's based on instinct. One of those moments when you know the world has tilted in your favor. The picture here was the first DJ took of me, at the SPCA. I remember, as I gently scratched the partition, he said, "Steve, there's a black lab." The Shadow Diaries were born.

Till next week. Thanks for reading.

Love, Shadow Baby

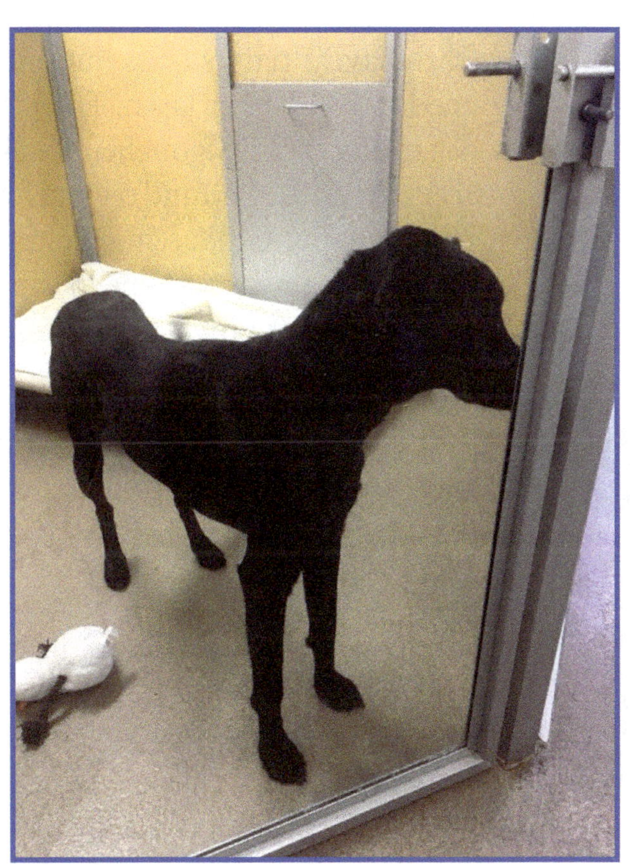

Diary Thirteen

Hi Everyone, it's Shadow. As you can see, I've been doing some thinking.

This week, DJ invented a new game, one I really like. He calls it Double Fetch.

I used to have 2 tennis balls but one of them bounced into the next lawn. Then this week the other one did! DS got them back, and so now I get to run around and try and fetch them both. It's fun, but exhausting! Thankfully my Daddies put out water for me in the yard. It's like I have 2 water bowls, too!

Which gets me thinking about 2s. First of all, that's my age! Also, I'm lucky to have 2 Daddies who are always making sure I'm loved. Which includes being fed...yup, you guessed it, twice a day!

My days are kind of like 2 in one. DJ is home most daytimes, and we get to do fun stuff. Then he leaves to go play with Kong (and I do, too). Hey, that's 2 Kongs! Then at night I get the second part of my day with DS.

Those are nice and quiet and snuggly.

DJ says I've learned a lot this week. I get TO go for walks. I usually get TWO treats. And on Sundays I get a special walk with both DS and DJ, TOO. DJ is a stickler for grammar! Cousin Jonathan Cornue would be proud!

But then nighttime comes. There are four different spots where I can sleep, but we all know that 4 is just 2 + 2. DJ says good, but math is not his subject.

But you want to know the best part? My 2 Daddies say that I'm one of a kind.

Till next week. Thanks for reading.

Love, Shadow Baby

"Tell your friends. *The Shadow Diaries* is the feel-good read of the year!"

--Minion, Miniature Pincher mix, Los Angeles, CA

Diary Fourteen

Hi Everyone, it's Shadow. I don't feel my best today, a stomach bug. DJ just says that makes me a true Pittman!

But I want to talk about happy stuff. You know what I like to do? Bounce. In the morning with DS or at night when DJ comes home, I like to put my front paws forward and bounce around. It's the puppy in me.

Know what else is fun? Some words sound like other words! Bounce becomes jounce, usually when I'm in the yard playing fetch. Ooh, I lift myself high off the ground, trying to catch the ball or just play with my Daddies.

I got a new toy this week. A frisbee. DS shared a video earlier this week of us tossing it around. I won the battle. Which means, again on rhyme, I trounced him.

But I'm perplexed when it comes to the end of my day. I've bounced and jounced and trounced all day, but what I really want to do is snuggle. That word doesn't match. So I'm inventing a new word. Because my favorite thing to do with DS and DJ is this: I like to snounce.

Thanks for reading. Hope I feel better!

Love, Shadow Baby

Diary Fifteen

Hi Everyone, it's Shadow. Thanks for all the concern last week. I'm more better than ever.

My house is filled with laughter. Well, and my barking. The first sound is fun, the second is loud. I can't help it, I'm a dog, and I think a pretty normal one. What dog doesn't go crazy when he sees a cat?

But as I've come to learn, I have some, what DJ says, quirks. That word makes me laugh. It has an onamonapia quality to it.

When I play catch, if the ball lands in the corner or side lawn areas, I won't retrieve it. Um, that's where I do my business. When I need to go out I jump off the sofa, do a fake stretch, run to the door and then retreat when DS opens it. I do a lap around the living room and then finally go out.

Another funny thing I do is when I'm eating. Oh, I love meal time (you all saw the video DS filmed). But I eat with such eagerness my bowl ends up halfway across the kitchen floor. See Exhibit A in the photo.

But even though I do those weird things, both DS and

DJ still laugh. Such a happy sound, which just gets my long tail wagging. DJ says it makes a TWAPP! sound, which he says is like something out of Batman. Then DS and DJ laugh again.

I think they're the quirky ones. I wouldn't have it any other way.

Thanks for reading.

Love, Shadow Baby

"I first met Shadow on Thanksgiving. I came to visit him at his house and boy, did we have a quick connection. Running and playing and cuddling on the sofa with his Dads and my Mom. He's cute, but then again, so am I. We might be dating now! I've been reading along every Sunday about Shadow's experiences. He had quite the eventful year! Lucky for all of you that you get to experience the world through his eyes. I'm just lucky that I can call him my bestie."

--Carter, Beagle, New York City

Diary Sixteen

Episode XVI: The Rise of Shadow

A few months ago, in a kennel far far away...

I came to live on my new planet with Two Daddies, and each morning I get to bark "you are my fathers." Then this force awakens, stretching my very long legs. Only a light saber (whatever that is) is longer.

I'm so eager for my walk that I can't wait. While DJ takes a shower I go into the bedroom and raid his shoes and socks. Uh, no, I don't chewy them with my jawas.

But the truth is I like feet. Pouncing with my paws, or licking DS's when we hang out on the couch watching a movie. DJ says I have a foot fetish. That doesn't make sense. Wouldn't it be a foot feetish? (DJ is resisting making a Boba Feet joke here.)

Anyway, I finally got my walk on the promenade this week, which opened up a whole new empire to me. Someday the waterfront will see a return of the Shadow.

Also this week I got to meet more of DS's buddies from school. Talk about a long time ago! Anyway, they called themselves the Shadow Demons, which kind of sounds menacing. But since they used my name, that makes me their master. I'm no phantom.

The fun part of living here is how different DJ and DS are. They are not clones. But each day they offer me a new hope. Oh, and to those who don't get this, don't seek revenge. That would be sithy.

Till next week, because this is not The Last Diary. (There, did I get them all?)

Love, Shadow Jedi

Diary Seventeen

Hi Everyone, it's Shadow. Hoppy Easter!

All week long on my walks I've seen lawn decorations of bunnies and eggs. Even my Daddies made eggs and colored them. I like the bright rainbow but I'm confused. Chickens make eggs. Not bunnies. Sometimes people have strange traditions.

But I'm happy to celebrate such a big holiday. DJ told me stories of remembrance, which is appropriate for this day of rebirth. First of all, there are the dogs that came before me. Both DS and DJ kept the collars and bandanna of Misty and Bongo. That's how I know I'm loved.

DJ also told me about his Dad. I think it's great he had such a good one. I think that's why he has such a big heart. Grandpa, who I never got to meet, loved Easter. He would preach and celebrate and wear purple robes!

That's kind of fitting, since purple is DS's favorite color. It just means our life is meant to be, colors illuminating our past and brightening our tomorrow.

But in the end I go back to those eggs. Since I like to eat, I want to try one. They are supposed to be healthy for my coat. Hey Daddies,

can I have the purple one?

Blessings to all as Spring brings a fresh hop to our lives.

Till next week,

Love, Shadow Baby

"Shadow and I have so much in common beyond being cousins. We know when our Dads need a snuggle—or, what Shadow calls, a snounce. He likes to make up words. During the day, we follow our Dads around and at night we fall asleep with them. The only difference is, Shadow wrote a book, but the good thing is, I got to read it, and it's full of hope and laughter. He reminds us of the bond between man and man's best friend. Don't miss this heartful and funny read."

--Ruby, Chesapeake Bay Retriever, Glenmont, NY

Diary Eighteen

Hi Everyone, it's Shadow, coming to you from Spring Break!

Gosh, this was a different kinda week, but from what DS says, this was just a preview of summer.

See, he didn't have to leave every morning like he usually does. So I got to see lots of DS!

Then there's DJ. Nothing was different. Does he ever not work? He still left to go play with that Kong all week. But we still did our daytime routine of walks and playtime, with the added bonus of DS being with us. That was fun. Lots of 3time!

Oh, speaking of fun, there were new games this week, and each one of us created one. DJ got 3 new balls and now we play Triple Fetch. DS runs around the yard with me, which gets me all excited. I race around in circles until I need a slurp of water. We need a name for that game.

Then there's the game I created: DJ calls it "Through the Legs." I go in between their legs but then stop before I get through. That's a signal to give my hind quarters a massage, which I love!

DJ was happy this week because his favorite band dropped a new album (whatever that means). He listened to it a lot and some of their other songs. One of them was Games People Play. But thankfully my Daddies also know Games Dogs Play.

Well, I guess that's it. I'm tired from playing. Spring Break sounds relaxing but it sure had its comings and goings. Gonna take a nap and get ready for a new adventure next week. Stay tuned....

Thanks for reading.

Love, Shadow Baby

Diary Nineteen

Special Edition

Hi Everyone, my name is Gustavo (but you can call me Gus). I'm the big handsome (so I'm told) Golden Retriever at the center of the first photo. I'm alongside my siblings Lucy and Marcy (the Beagles). I'm here to report that my cousin Shadow is fine.

But what a whirlwind of a week. This is what I learned. Shadow's week started out normal, walks and playing and eating food. It all changed on Friday. See, DS and DJ had to go out of town for 2 days. So Shadow had to stay at a doggie hotel.

Hmm, he didn't like not being in his home. He missed his routine and he sure missed his Daddies. DS and DJ came to visit us and even stayed overnight. We sat and cuddled and they told us all about Shadow. I was like, "wait, of the Shadow Diaries fame?" Wow, our parents have read those to us!

Anyway, it's my pleasure to guest host for Shadow while he's away. Kind of like when Johnny Carson (whoever that is) would take time off and let someone else

host! (Uncle DJ made me write that). He sure has silly references!

But I'm happy to write that Shadow is happily back home after his dogcation and is so busy playing and eating and snouncing that he let me take the reins of the diary this week.

In the end, it all came full circle. On the day Shadow came to his forever home it was raining really hard. And you know what? It was raining today when he came back home. Guess you can't spell rainbow without it!

Well, thanks Shadow for letting me and Lucy and Marcy help out! Nice to see your new picture from when you got home. Glad you are loved. Go get a smother hug from DS and DJ.

Thanks for reading. Now back to our regularly scheduled programming.

Love, Gustavo (Baby!)

Diary Twenty

Hi Everyone, it's Shadow. I'm back!!

Rain. Cold. Wind. It's a terrible day outside. But I still needed my walk. DJ and I got pretty wet. But at least there was no cyclone to whip us away to another land!

Speaking of other places, last weekend I stayed in an Oz...I mean, odd placc. It's not that I was a coward at the doggie hotel but my heart was racing and my brain kept wondering where DS and DJ were.

But they came for me and all is back to normal. DJ took me for my daily walks and he kept singing some song as I happily reunited with the cute kids next door, with dogs Milo and Wally and Bea and Rusty, plus the nice florist lady around the corner.

DS took me for a grooming, even though I was nervous getting in the car again. The friendly lady I met gave me a pedicure! And I got a new toy, a blue squeaky football! I love playing with that.

But back to that song DJ was singing. It's called "Who are the people in your neighborhood." He says it's from Sesame Street. I don't know how to get there. But

it sure was nice to be among my friends again.

Which brings me back to my original thought this week. It's really simple: "There's No Place Like Home."

Thanks for reading, and also thanks to Gus, Lucy and Marcy for helping out with last week's diary.

Love, Shadow Baby

"*The Shadow Diaries* is one rescue dog's journey to finding out what home really means, and the infinite amount of love that defines it. Shadow, DJ, and DS invite you into their family and share a delightful tail that is paws-itively sure to have you smiling from ear-to-ear."

--Sadie, Jack Russell/Maltese, New York City

Diary Twenty-One

Hi Everyone, it's Shadow. Or at least, I think it is. Let me explain.

"A rose by any other name would smell as sweet," wrote Shakespeare (whoever he is!). He sure was right because I like to smell all sorts of flowers.

But what that quote really got me thinking about was the idea of a name. Once upon a time someone named me Shadow. I'm not sure I remember anymore who. DJ and DS sure are curious to know, but that's not easy to communicate with a bark.

My Daddies were happy with my name. It fits me. Especially last week, DJ said, because I followed him all the time! And DS and I snuggled a lot. Sometimes they don't see me behind them. Aren't you always supposed to see your shadow?

But I've noticed that I have other names that are said all the time. Some I understand: Sweet Boy, Baby, Good Boy, Bouncy Boy, Cute Boy, and of course, Shadow Baby. Some I don't get: Shadowkins and Babykins. I don't know what a kin is, but at least they are said with a laugh.

Then there are names that sound more like adjectives:

nutcase, crazy, goofy. I hear those mostly when I'm running around the house or the yard with my doggie energy. Who knows, maybe I'm all these names, with more to come.

I want to close this week talking about the photo I attached. Look in the background and you'll see two photographs. DS told me about one of them, his parents. Walter and Marie. Then DJ told me about Jerry and Rosemary, his parents. They too had and have lots of names. Mom, Dad, Grandma, Grandpa. They're even called Great.

This past week would have been the 72nd anniversary for my Syracuse grandparents. Wow, Grandma Rosemary Pittman, what a great love story that lives forever. Imagine that in dog years! What I like best is your name, because it's spelled with a rose. Sweet.

Well, I wrote a lot this week, so I guess it's time for a nap. Till next week.

Love, Shadow Baby, et al (whatever that means)

Diary Twenty-Two

Hi Everyone, it's Shadow. No, that first photo is not me. But it symbolizes my feelings this week.

Every day I play fetch and sometimes I miss the ball and it goes rolling over to the memorial marker for my brother, Bongo. DJ always exclaims, "Ooh, Bongo got that one."

When DJ comes home from work at King Kong, he's always talking about the service dogs and K-9 units who help keep his theatre safe. What a great thing those men and dogs do— dedicated to those they are sworn to protect.

It's Memorial Day, and instead of summer and beaches and relaxation (DJ says whatever that is) I'm thinking about all the other dogs who lived their lives in service to the happiness of others.

DS has spoken a lot about Bongo and how the two of them shared a life based on a needed renewal. Did you know DS had two other dogs before him? Beagles named Josh and Jessey. DS sure loves his puppies!

DJ talks too about Misty. She was his dog when he was a kid, during a time when he learned the joys and rewards of canine companionship. For 14 years, Misty gave light to dark nights. DJ doesn't so much remember the family's earlier dog, Tuffy.

There have been other dogs in our family who remain in our hearts. DJ mentioned so many names! Bozo (that sounds like a clown!) and Bentley and Barney. There was Rudy and Cassie, Bear and Riley (who looked more like a hyena!) Oh, and fluffy Teddy and that numnut, Summer! Bowie (who DJ had fun dog sitting with), Maggie and Gatsby, Der Hund, Ebbie, Penelope, and of course Misty's cousin, Lady. All sweet dogs who are remembered.

DJ has one more dog he wishes to talk about. Once upon a time there was a dog named Aggie, a beautiful Doberman mix who could be cuddly sweet but who sometimes couldn't control his impulses. Poor Aggie was unwell and when he passed, DJ struck out on a solo journey that didn't take a canine curve until he met DS and Bongo. They set him down a new path.

So, on this weekend, for all the dogs who have crossed that bridge, may your forever lives be filled with all the vibrant colors of the rainbow. Know the impact you all had. It's because of your sunset that I live, not in the shadows, but under a golden sun.

Memorial Day. Life's tomorrow is nothing without it's yesterday.

Thanks for reading.

Love, Shadow Baby

Diary Twenty-Three

Hi Everyone, it's Shadow. Let's celebrate! I even have my party hat on. DJ says it wasn't easy getting it to stay on!

Anyway, the past couple of weeks I've had lots on my mind, so today I wanted to get back to my regular routine and maybe have a little bit of fun. It's also a new month and I hear if you say "rabbits" it's good luck. Even better, I saw a real bunny on my walk yesterday.

June is off to a good start. Tomorrow is DS's Birthday! Wow. From all I've heard, last year was a big one and DS threw a fun party with so many guests! I would have enjoyed being there, too. I could have met so many of you!

But life and fate are on their own schedule, so I'm here for this year's celebration. DJ told me how lucky I am to have DS as Daddy 1! I know. We spend so many nights together, he makes me feel like home is the best place ever. DJ said I was right.

This last week we enjoyed a holiday, so both DS and DJ were home. Then we had company. Audrey and Steve (hey, he has the same name as DS!). They came to the house and I cuddled with them and played in the yard. I could tell DJ was so happy to see them.

Tonight, I'll see more friends as we celebrate DS's new year. I'm sure I'll bounce and pounce when our friends arrive. It's what I do. I get excited when people come over. I'm also hoping to get cake but probably DJ will just give me a treat.

Birthdays are special. You get a chance to think about where you've been and where you're going. It's been an amazing year for DS. He's going to be 51! I can't even do the math in dog years. But there is so much more to look forward to. I hear there's a wedding (whatever that is) coming up.

I guess what I'm saying is life is an endless celebration. Small moments like when we enjoy our 3time, or when there's a holiday, or a birthday or an epic party. You run and play in the moment, always knowing there's another candle to add to the cake.

Yup, I'm still thinking about cake.

Thanks for reading. Until next week....

Love, Shadow Baby

Diary Twenty-Four

Sing-a-Long Edition

Hi Everyone, it's Shadow.

My home is alive, with The Sound of Music. So, it's got me thinking about my favorite things. First, raindrops on roses? Sure, that sounds nice. Second, whiskers on kittens. Yeah, not so much. But there's so much that makes my life full! As they say in the theatre, cue the music...Curtain Up!

"Meal time, fresh water
And treats all day long
Blue plastic footballs that squeak at my touch
Balls in bright colors that bounce in my mouth
These are a few of my doggiest things

DS and DJ
And snouncing till dawn
Barking at showers and dashing up stairs
Walks in the morning and sometimes at night

These are a few of my doggiest things

DS in purple
And DJ in blue
Plans for the future bound to come true
Family and friends and a wedding in weeks
These are a few of my doggiest things.

When the cat prowls
When the storm hits
When the mail arrives
I simply remember my Daddies are home
And then I just feeeeel....so glad!"

Happy Tony Awards Day! (Whatever those are.) P.S. Congrats to my buddy KONG (pictured here) on his Special Award. Hope you win more!

Thanks for singing along (you know you did!).

Love, Shadow (Broadway) Baby

Diary Twenty-Five

Hi Everyone, it's Shadow. I have a story to tell.

PROLOGUE: His name was Velo, a sleek greyhound who ran as fast as the wind. He lived in a small town in Upstate New York. There might have been a windmill (whatever that is!). He would run through the village, always in search of something. His owners didn't know what. But I know. It was a black Labrador named Bella. They liked each other and they gave birth to a litter of pups.

CHAPTER ONE: One of them was adopted by a young family. They couldn't resist him. They took one look at this soft-coated, short-haired, black-as-midnight puppy—one who followed them around everywhere—and named him Shadow. Gotta say, it was a pretty perfect name. They loved his gentle nature.

CHAPTER TWO: Anyway, this newly named pup was taken from the small town and became part of a new family. In an apartment in New Jersey! (Wherever that is!) There was a Dad, a Mom, two kids, and to his delight, another dog. His name was Miles and he was white, a direct contrast, and he was little. But back then so too was this Shadow boy. The home wasn't the largest, so sofa space was at a premium. They had to snuggle close. But that was ok. Shadow stayed warm.

CHAPTER THREE: It was nice having a new Dad. He took him for walks. He played with him. But he always had a distant look on his face. It was especially sad when he came to talk to Shadow and said, "We love you, sweet boy, but we cannot keep you. Our landlord said you're getting too big." The only words Shadow understood back then was walk, eat, play, snuggle. He didn't want to leave. Surely not from this second father he'd known.

CHAPTER FOUR: Shadow went to live in a shelter, and even though they took good care of him, he knew his life had changed. What would tomorrow bring? Well, it took eight tomorrows, and a bit of a hunger strike, until these two cute men (his perspective, but he's not wrong) came and said hi. They fell in love, and you know what, so did Shadow. What a bonus! Two New Daddies!

EPILOGUE: Shadow lives in a house now. There's no windmill, but life sure has its share of rotations. Marking the passage of time and deepening the bond established on that first day. Sure, Shadow has had his share of ups and down, but when he stops to think about it, mostly when he's alone and staring out the window at the world he's seen, he thinks how blessed he's been. He's had four fathers.

DJ keeps telling me he writes books and likes to make up stories. Some are based in reality, while some are pure fiction. I like to believe that the truth falls somewhere in between.

Happy Father's Day to DS and DJ. They sure were lucky to have had their Dads. Which makes me all the luckier. You live by example. You love from the heart.

Thanks for reading my new story.

Love, Shadow Baby

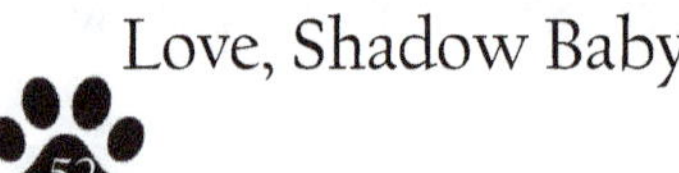

Diary Twenty-Six

Hi Everyone, it's Shadow. It's been a long journey to this point. 26 is a big number. That's half a year. Or in my world, 3 ½ years! There's only one word on my mind and that word is WOW!

Okay, that's not entirely true, especially for regular readers of my diary. I often have lots to say. But this week I think I'm going to keep my thoughts short and simple. Maybe I'll let DS and DJ take over the laptop.

DJ: Shadow, you make me laugh. The way you play with your toys. The way we play triple fetch together. The way we walk and the way we talk to each other. Yes, I speak words and you, well, you bark (sometimes a lot), but what we're thinking is always conveyed through our eyes. You have such an intuition, a way of staring into the soul. You know when I'm happy. You know when I'm sad. You know just when to cuddle and make it all right. Snuggling all night has become snouncing at night—your word!

DS: I'm sitting and watching our sweet Shadow as you lie comfortably on the living room couch, staring at me with your sensitive amber eyes. You are

as comfortable in this home as DJ and I are. We are a small family, and the three of us enrich each other daily. Shadow, you bring sweetness, spunk (read: pouncy) humor and cuddle time to your Daddies. After a rough work day, you manage to make us smile when you greet us at the door, or lower our blood pressures when we're unwinding. One of life's pleasures is caressing your soft fur and sensing our mutual affection. As I gaze back at you again, your eyes have now closed – yup, it's nap time. I can stare at you for hours. All the while feeling thankful and blessed that the three of us have been lucky enough to have found the same path. There's much love and laughter in our 3time Forever Home.

Gosh my Daddies had a lot to say. But I love it. They are always on the run. Working, having fun (hey, without me!), watching movies and listening to music and laughing a lot (yay, with me!). They are so special and have given me the happiest home I could have ever envisioned. Yup, that's a big word. DJ taught it to me. Cause he too can't believe this life he leads. He didn't envision it either.

What's best about where I live? I'm comfortable. I'm safe. I'm always well fed, I get smother-hugged daily. DJ tells me my stories may end up in a book someday. (He knows a few things about books!) Me, I like to spread the simplest of messages. It's not just about being loved. It's about feeling secure. I took a leap of faith 6 months ago. DJ tells me he once took one too.

You know what we each got from that leap? We got DS. DJ says don't change a thing. Yeah, that.

Thanks for reading. There's so much more to come. WOW.

Love, Shadow Baby

Diary Twenty-Seven

Hi Everyone, it's Shadow. I enter the second half of this year thinking about a special word: Pride. Everyone likes to take pride in who they are and what they do. We are all an array of colors that span the spectrum of life.

So, the word pride got me curious. DJ helped me do an online search (whatever that means). Here's one definition: "Confidence and self-respect as expressed by members of a group, typically one that has been socially marginalized on the basis of their shared identity, culture, and experience."

Experience is the path of life, with acceptance leading the way. Both ideas have brought me here. Let me tell you about my home, my experience, and my 2 Daddies. We share everything, whether in the moment or told through memory. Each of us approaches life in different ways, each with a common goal. Happiness.

So, DS. You are awesome. You wear pride like a second skin. You are passionate and committed to all you believe in. You attend parades and rallies. You speak out about injustice and you breathe equality. You put on hats draped in purple and T-shirts that spread your message of unity. You are brave. You teach lessons beyond a classroom.

So, DJ. You are quieter in your strength. But you've come a long way. You live your life through words, even while knowing there are those around you who oppose the message. You are forceful in your own way, never letting anyone deny you what matters most. Yup, you set an example by just being yourself in a world defined by diversity. You know, simply, that we all belong.

Our home is filled with color. Orange and yellow and green and red and purple (lots of purple!) and pink and blue and every other hue. But that's how it should be. Life isn't black and white. Even me, I may only be dark in color, but my eyes see a world in shades filled with love and respect for all.

Happy Pride to DS and DJ. Boy, did I hit the jackpot with 2 Daddies who realize the world is better when it's enriched by the understanding that differences are the true constant. Be you.

Thanks for reading. Hug someone.

Love, Shadow Baby

Diary Twenty-Eight

Hi everyone, it's Shadow. Boy, is it warm outside!

But have you ever heard of Christmas in July? It's a silly idea, and of course there's no snow. (Unless you live in Syracuse, because that could happen.)

July is supposed to celebrate independence. So why do people think about the wintery holiday that's six months away? I found out, so let me explain by telling you a story. It's about Rudolph and Hermey and DJ and DS. And ultimately (isn't it always) about me.

DJ first came to what is now our home in July of 2016. Wow, that's three years ago! He and DS were still getting to know each other, and as DJ says, for a Manhattanite to come to the Jersey Shore was...different. See, DJ had always kind of lived an independent life in that big city. Feeling different. Like a reindeer with a red nose.

On the other side of the Hudson River (wherever that is), there was DS. Looking, hoping, for that next phase of life. Of love. So, DJ came to visit, on, of all days, July 4th. They actually skipped the fireworks down in Asbury Park, even though watching them had been the plan. But the truth is the fireworks had already gone off. They realized something special was happening.

But then something more special happened. Stopped at a red light, they started talking about silly interests of theirs. They found a common one. DJ confessed his love for the classic Christmas special Rudolph the Red-Nosed Reindeer. DS admitted his own love of it. And then, DJ started imitating all the characters' voices, and, in a moment of laughter, they stared into each other's eyes and saw that gifts are given all year 'round.

And how do I fit into this story? There's a classic line where Rudolph and elf/dentist-wannabe Hermey state that they can be independent together. Sounds like an oxymoron to me (I know, I keep learning big words!). But I kinda feel that way too. I sometimes like to seek out my own path lined with silver and gold. Does that make me Yukon Cornelius? I think so, because wasn't Yukon part of the 3team that ended the Bumble's reign?

Christmas in July? it does exist.

Thanks for reading.

Love, Shadow Baby

Diary Twenty-Nine

Hi Everyone, it's Shadow. Ok, let's dive into the deep end.

I'm learning more about words. Did you know some have multiple meanings? Take, for instance, my name. Sure, that's what people call me, but it can also be the dark shape on the sidewalk when the sun hits you right. Or it can be someone who follows you all the time. Three different meanings but somehow you still end up with me.

Here's another word: shower. Every morning when DJ goes to take one, he draws open the glass doors and turns on the nozzle. You know what I do? I bark a lot and I pounce my paws (video attached). I'm not sure why. DJ sure looks brave when he steps behind those doors and lets the water soak him. I do the same routine at night when DS goes behind those glass doors.

But in recent weeks I've heard the word shower used in a different context. I've uncovered what it means to "shower" someone, whether it's with gifts or affection. It sounds like a really nice thing. When DS was still at school (whatever that is), his friends and coworkers planned a fun party and they had cake and gave cards and gifts and hugs. Then at his other school (hey, why does

he get 2?), other people did the same thing. That's super great.

Today turned out to be DJ's turn. His city friends held a party for him, and DS was there, too! Again, there was cake and gifts and lots of laughter, because DJ likes to laugh. He always says I make him laugh. I like that. But after the fun, after the hugs and congratulations (I guess there's a big event coming up soon), DJ had a private moment. A silent appreciation, for friendship and support and understanding.

But here's where I get confused. When DJ or DS goes in the shower, they get soaked all over. But when they have one of these parties, the only water that escapes seeps from their eyes. A shower may cleanse the body, but the other kind of shower opens the heart. Humans are as complex as the words they use.

Humans. That's another word with so many meanings. But the only one that matters to me is that of protector. And because I feel so lucky to have DJ and DS taking care of me, you know what I'm going to do? I'm going to shower them with licks and kisses and my special snounces.

In the end, whether it's in my bowl or streaming out of a shower or displayed through tears, water has one meaning: life.

Thanks for reading. And thanks, too, to everyone for making DS and DJ feel special. I do what I can. You sure did yours.

Love, Shadow Baby

Diary Thirty

Hi Everyone, it's Shadow. Summer is in full swing. Let's play!

And boy did I play this week! See, I got this new toy and it's a lot of fun. It's called a GoDogGo, and it spews out six balls in succession (whatever that means). Then you're supposed to catch the balls. DJ seems to be having more fun with it than me, since he keeps catching the balls in his hands. Me, I'd use my mouth if I could trace their trajectory. (Big phrase!) Usually I just pounce on them!

Thanks to Aunt Elizabeth Pittman Keene and Uncle Douglas Keene for visiting and bringing me this toy. They told me their doggies Buster and Baxter used to play with it. I like that I have older cousins, so that way I get such fun hand-me-downs!

It's been a blisteringly hot week, so I've had to stay hydrated and be inside more than I like. But I still get my morning walk. Each day this week it seemed my walk got earlier and earlier, but hey, I'm smart. The sun hasn't risen so high in the sky yet. What's fun about my walk is I get to play with (read: lunge at) the neighborhood cats and bunnies. But then the big dogs bark at me! Kind of puts life in perspective.

I'm not alone in playing this summer. DS is enjoying his summer break from school, doing his art, watching movies and going out to dinner with friends. We even filmed some fun videos for the start of his school year. I'm a star! As for DJ, playtime is limited, because he's still going into the city most days to work with that monkey. Drink lots of water. I mean, I wouldn't want DJ to faint!

But in the end, I realize you can't play all the time. Sure, we play indoors a lot right now, especially when I grab my blue squeezy football and go running up and down the stairs. And then up and down the stars again. That routine is on heavy rotation (whatever that means). I've got to use up my puppy energy somehow. It's nice though to cuddle among the pillows on my sofa and take a nap. I'm a dog. I need my rest.

As the day winds down, though, even though I'm cool in my air-conditioned house, a bit of warmth is always welcome. That's when I realize it's time to relax and snounce with DS and DJ. Playtime can sometimes equal quiet time. I let out a big yawn and then I'm at peace.

Finally, that big day is approaching for my Daddies. Tune in next week for the start of a special series of entries, what I'm calling The Wedding Trilogy.

Thanks for reading.

Love, Shadow Baby

Diary Thirty-One

The Wedding Trilogy, Part One

Hi Everyone, it's Shadow. It's only the biggest party ever! DS and DJ are getting hitched, and I'm going to try and sum up the festivities. But it's gonna take three entries. Because to tell a story the right way, you need a beginning, a middle, and a future.

Let's start at the very beginning....hey, wait, that sounds like the opening of a song. We sure had tons of fun doing a sing-a-long a bunch of diaries ago. So, back by popular demand (whatever that means), let's sing another song to tell the origins of how we became...well, you'll see.

"Here's the story

Of a man named DJ

Who was living in a shoebox in the sky

He worked daytime

And nights and weekends

He dined on Chinese Food

"Here's the story

Of a man named DS

Who was living just a few miles from the shore

He taught small kids,

Then painted pictures

But he so wanted more

"Then this one day these two guys met each other

And later got a sweet and cuddly pooch

Now in one week,

Their love's official

That's the way that they became the Shadow Bunch.

"The Shadow Bunch

The Shadow Bunch

That's the way we became One Family"

(Dun uh da dun da...)

"And Peggy Pittman Menter as Alice"

Haha! That was fun. Thanks for singing along. Hard to resist that tune! Part Two comes next week. DS and DJ's Big Day!

Love, Shadow Baby

Diary Thirty-Two

The Wedding Trilogy, Part Two

Hi Everyone, its Shadow. Well, it's here. Gosh, my Daddies are gonna get married. But even though the ceremony doesn't happen until the afternoon, there's still so much to tell you about. The events of the past week that led up to this moment have kinda been like the storm before the calm.

I could feel the excitement in the air after I posted the last entry. So many likes, thanks! A sense of anticipation, of building to a crescendo. (Yup, my new word of the week). DS has been home mostly, quietly going about his plans. DJ has still had to work his shifts with the monkey and also, he sure does pace around a lot! I'm energetic and like to run throughout the house but DJ, can you sit down and relax?

Friday was a fun day for my Daddies. Each of them had friends in town for the Big Day, and they got to meet up in that Big City called Manhattan. DS and his friends went to see a show about someone named Cher (which is an appropriate name since three people share the role!). And DJ's friends came to see the monkey, DJ was really happy to welcome them, not only to the show but to this celebratory weekend.

So today is the Day. I won't be there in person (in dog?) but I understand and I'll watch the video later. I've been told I'm high maintenance (whatever that means) and in the end, DS and DJ need their special moment. I know all three of us will have many days of happiness in the coming days, weeks, and dog years. In the meantime, I get to hang out with a nice lady who is called a dog-sitter. Hope she likes to play because I got more new toys!

But as much as the Big Day is all about today, for me, yesterday was da bomb (Do the kids still say that?) Because...it happened! The moment I've been waiting for. She was here. SHE. The Matriarch herself. The grand and great lady. Grandma Rosemary Pittman. She came to my house and she was sweet and kind and she pet me and gave

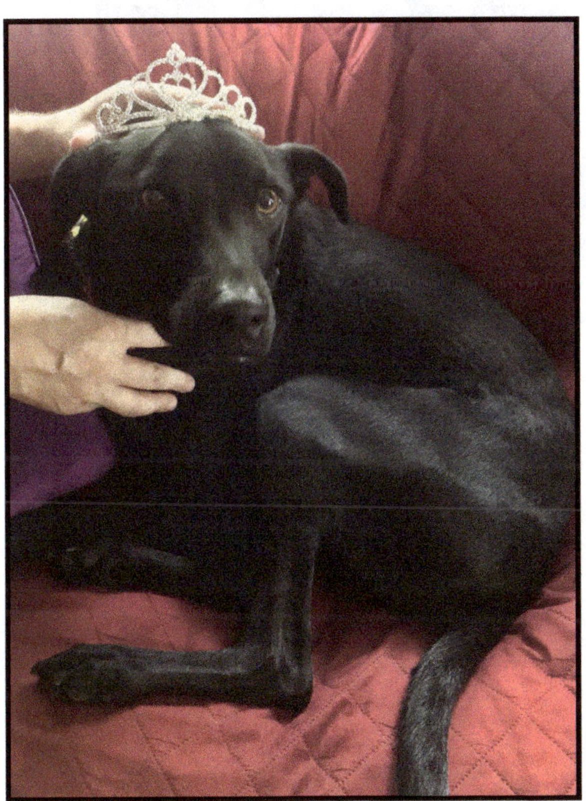

me a treat and told me what a good boy I am. I even wore a tiara in anticipation!

Lots of other friends and family stopped by too and we played and laughed and ate and I pounced about. The excitement was palpable. (Okay, guess I've got two new words this week.) I'll be thinking of my Daddies all day today, knowing that what they are experiencing comes once in a lifetime. Love may be just another word in the dictionary, but it's definition could fill its own volume.

Thanks for reading. Tune in next week for the recap of an awesome day and a peek at the future.

Love, Shadow Baby

IT IS USELESS

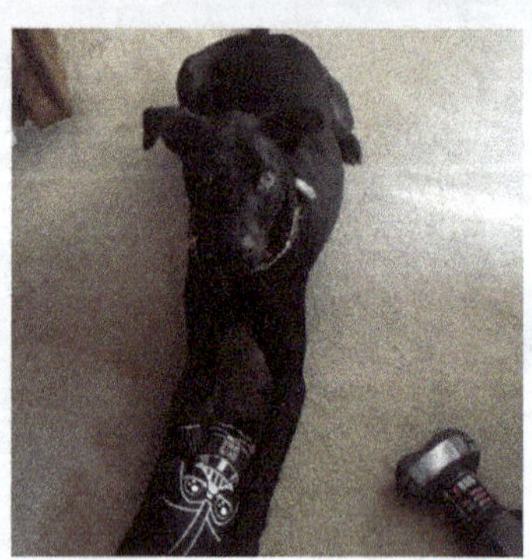

Diary Thirty-Three

The Wedding Trilogy, Part Three

Hi Everyone, it's Shadow. Wow, what a party!

I ran around with my dog-sitter, inside the house and in the yard. We played with all my toys, including a new one that looks like Darth Vader (whoever he is!) and another that is shaped like a bone but is soft and fluffy. Tug of war, fetch, bouncing and pouncing. Lots of treats, too! I was so exhausted that when it was time to sleep, I curled up with the nice lady and we drifted off.

DJ and DS who?

Haha! I know, you all really want to know about their wedding. All the details about the ceremony and the reception and the after-party. The last part DJ says is a Pittman family tradition and tends to go late. And boy, were there a lot of my Pittman family in attendance! DS also saw relatives he had not seen in a while and his bright smile showed how happy he was knowing they were there. And so many friends from near and far, all of them traveling to celebrate my Daddies.

I've seen lots of pictures and wow, did DJ and DS look handsome in their suits. I've never see them dressed up like that. At home it's always casual, shorts T-shirts. Imagine if DJ took me for my morning walk in his Armani! Then again, he'd steal all the attention and we all know that's not happening. Our Keyport enclave (this

week's big word) is pure Shadowland. DS looked resplendent in his purple. That color I see on him a lot! I should call him Prince DS.

There were special moments, like when DS spoke his vows and then DJ followed with his. There were some great laughs and I hear someone named an officiant tried to plagiarize my diary! "A Reading from the Book of Shadow."! Hey, get your own act! (Actually, it was really funny and got the ceremony off to a great start.) There were emotional moments, remembrances of people who live in spirit, and then there were tears. Happy ones.

I have a feeling life around 20 May is going to calm down a bit now. DS still has a whole month before school starts up again. He'll probably do his art and watch a ton of movies. DJ has only 1 week remaining with the monkey and then I think I'm going to be seeing a lot more of him. For me that's a good thing. For DS, too. I know DJ will be working hard then on getting my diary a book deal!

In the meantime, we're all exhausted. I'm going to rest up and it may take a while. Maybe this doggie needs some quiet time away from the computer. So, I may ask one of my friends to guest host next week. I sent out a bark requesting help and I'm waiting to hear back. I know I will. I have good hearing.

Thanks to everyone who made DJ and DS's special day super and amazing and joyful. That's what counts. As much as hearts swell, you know what? There's always room for more love.

See you in two weeks.

Love, Shadow Baby

Diary Thirty-Four

Special Guest Host Edition

Hi Everyone, it's King Kong. My buddy Shadow is letting me take over his diary this week because, well, he's tired after writing the Wedding Trilogy. Plus, I'm skipping town and he's giving me a chance to say goodbye. See, today is my last show on Broadway.

You may be asking, what do Shadow and Kong have in common? Simple. A guy who Shadow calls DJ, one I call Ticket Taker Joe (now TTJ). I first met TTJ last October and for the first few weeks it was a rocky relationship. I still had some rehearsals to do. I heard it's called previews (whatever that means).

But once we opened in November, life became fun and exciting. I always liked when TTJ came down to the lip of the stage before the show to say hi. We wouldn't talk and instead just stare at each other. We always knew what our eyes were saying. Kinda like how TTJ and Shadow interact.

See, Shadow came into TTJ and DS's (I've heard so much about him!) life a couple months later, in December. I've always felt a kinship with that cute dog. He may bark and I may roar, but somehow we could communicate across the miles. Animals (even when they're puppets) have a bond that goes beyond human understanding.

I've had a great time in New York. The audiences have been so enthusiastic, even

while some of them have been scared. I didn't mean to do that. I was just acting. And some nights, when I was nervous, it was always nice to see that door to the orchestra open and I'd see TTJ standing in the back. He would smile and encourage me. Sending me the strength to climb the Empire State Building.

Before my show closes, I would be remiss in not acknowledging DS. He came to see me once and I hear he thought I turned in a Tony-worthy performance. And guess what? I did. I won a Special Tony. But what DS mostly did was support TTJ. It's not easy coming into the city to work eight shows a week. There were some days TTJ was gone for 14 hours, and I know he was missing Shadow as much as Shadow was missing him. DS was always there, playing with Shadow and picking up TTJ at the train station late at night. Thanks, DS.

Well, I guess I should, like my show, wrap this up. Shadow, I'm imagining you and me hanging out, maybe having a meal or drink together. Just the two of us. I would order a banana daiquiri, and you, maybe you would just slurp water and think it's Daddy Juice. We would clink our glasses and cheer the unique connection we shared this past year.

I think our meeting would take place at a Chinese restaurant. To celebrate my next big move to Shanghai. I'll miss you. TTJ says he'll miss me. That's the beauty of memories. They never leave us.

And with one last ROAR, I exit, stage north.

Love, King Kong Baby

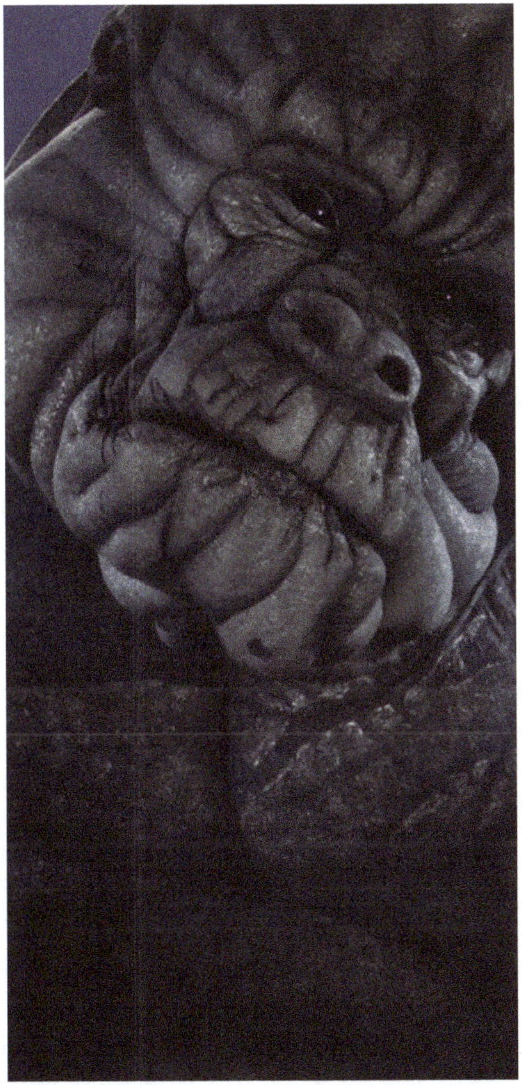

Diary Thirty-Five

Hi Everyone, it's Shadow. Welcome to the Dog Days of Summer!

As I reach this thirty-fifth edition of my diary, it seems like it will never end. (Hey, no agreeing, you love reading it!). But that got me thinking of summer and how when we approach the end of August the heat gets...over-heated. I'm getting ready for some cool breezes.

But the phrase, "Dog Days," had me wondering what it meant. After all, I am a dog. As I panted after a walk and a recent game of triple fetch, DJ could tell I was getting tired. I communicated to him that it might be better to go inside and find out where such an odd phrase came from.

Here's what we learned.

The Dog Days refers to the brightest proper star in the universe, also known, in Latin, as *dies caniculares*. It refers to the hottest, sultriest (whatever that means) days of the season. We've had our share for sure. Did you know it also coincides with the heliacal (this week's big word, which means sunrise!) rising of the Dog

Star, Sirius? And Sirius is also a song by DJ's favorite band. It's like looking at an Eye in the Sky.

But, ssshhh.... don't tell DS that we're ready for Autumn. To him it means back to work, back to school, back to waking up early. But that's still a week away. So, DS can continue with his present schedule, hearing about my morning walks chasing bunnies and cats rather than being on them! That's okay, I got night-time walks from him when DJ was playing with the monkey.

Oh, I would be remiss in not thanking King Kong for writing his brilliant substitute diary last week. I wish him well, and while I know DJ will miss certain aspects of his regular schedule, it sure is nice that he doesn't have to leave six days a week to ride that rattling train. I like having him home. Saturday, we sat out in the yard, he was reading and I was chomping on a toy. It's gonna be a few more months before we hear more stories from the west side.

Life is about adventures. Never knowing what the next day will bring. DS knows that his weeks with the school kids always come with surprises, and DJ is constantly entertained by the twists and turns of his novels. It's nice to see him back full-time at the computer crafting his latest mystery. I may have a cameo in this one!

But as much as the unexpected is a slice of life, so too is routine. That's what I offer to my Daddies. Consistency is the backbone of any day. Meal time, walk time, play time, sleep time. DS and DJ (especially DJ!) could take a page out of my book (diary?) and learn that not every minute needs to be planned. Some minutes are special in the fact that you stopped to sniff the flowers.

Yup, August is ending soon, Summer's on the wane. New adventures await us. But for now, I like being home and love having DS and DJ there at the same time. Lots of relaxing 3time, a chance to stare at the night sky and bark at the moon. I may

just see my canine companion twinkling back at me.

Thanks for reading. I had fun researching this one.

Love, Shadow Baby

"My Dad, Neil S. Plakcy writes The Golden Retriever Mystery series, so if he knows anything, it's books...and dogs. *The Shadow Diaries* is a book suffused with joy. This memoir details the black lab's first year in his new household. It's told in Shadow's voice as he explores his world with enthusiasm. DS is an artist and teacher, and DJ an author and Broadway ticket taker. Since their work schedules are opposite, there's usually at least one human around to play with Shadow. There are lots of humorous bits about Shadow's learning human terms, and the growing affection between the three of them. It's a book that all dog lovers will enjoy."

--Brody, Golden Retriever, Hollywood, FL

Diary Thirty-Six

Hi Everyone, it's Shadow. It's a double holiday weekend! Bet you didn't know that.

Sure, it's Labor Day, which celebrates American workers and does so in an ironic way: by declaring Monday as a day off. Today is also National K-9 Security Dog Day. Gosh, you all sure do like to celebrate your special holidays with 3-day weekends. It's almost like people don't want to work!

But I know we need to work, and in my home, work is in a constant juxtaposition (another big word!) for both DS and DJ. This coming Tuesday, DS heads back to school. DJ, meanwhile, he's home, his theatre having gone dark for a bit. So, I go from one being home and the other gone, to the other being home and the one being away. Hmm, I wonder if that sentence makes sense! English is a silly language. I just bark. Somehow they know what I'm saying.

While we celebrate our work ethic and acknowledge a day of relaxation, I'd like to talk about that other holiday I mentioned. Where we celebrate the K-9 units! Dogs do special things. They make you laugh, sure, because we like to walk and pounce and snuggle (snounce!), but we also know we sometimes have a different mission. You feed us and you love us. What we do is protect you. A job based on both instinct and training.

So, on this Labor Day, let's thank all the dogs on patrol. Still working, despite

the fact it's a human holiday. Keeping us safe, along with their handlers who keep them happy. It's an uncertain world out there, and to know man and dog—best friends—do what they do together is testament to our bond. I mean, I've never heard of a C-9 Unit! (Though supposedly those felines have that number of lives! Yikes!)

As I've learned, this is a weekend to take a breather (see photo!). Sit back before gearing up for a new season. DS and DJ had their final week of summer, not quite a honeymoon but some nights were lit by the magic of time spent together. They got to hang out in the pool in Asbury Park (wherever that is) and meet friends for drinks and dinner. I got to meet new friends and visit with family, too. I took my first road trip! More on that next week.

Maybe Labor Day is the perfect way to end the summer. Recognizing the work that you do, but also knowing work is not the constant but rather the means to your happiness. When you come home, you have a snack, a beverage, a meal, and if you're lucky, you get to pet a cute dog at the door. One that is so happy to see you, tail thwapping.

Work is conditional. Love, well that's unconditional. Both help shape an ideal life.

Thanks, as always, for reading my latest entry.

Love, Shadow Baby

Diary Thirty-Seven

Hi Everyone, it's Shadow. Guess what? I had my first road trip!

But first, DJ had to sit me down and tell me what a road trip was. You get in the car and you drive for a long time. You know what? It was so much fun!

See, we went to visit the Keene's. They're that nice family (Aunt Liz and Uncle Doug) that came to visit me and brought me the GoDogGo toy. Now I got to go to their house. It was in another state, Pennsylvania (wherever that is!) I'd heard of their dogs—Buster and Baxter, two Cockapoo brothers. I'm not sure our interaction went so well in the beginning. Buster and I said hello, but in our growly enthusiasm, my Batman bandanna got ripped. DJ got me a new one. Baxter was cute and kind of hung out in the background.

But wow, there was a fenced-in yard covered with grass and I got to run around and play and jump and just indulge my inner dog. Then we went for a walk in the neighborhood. It was peaceful and quiet as all three of us dogs smelled and sniffed the lawns and the trees and the air and trotted about. (See the photo!) I think that was my favorite part! You all know how I love

my walks.

DS did the driving both ways. On the morning ride, I stared out the window and observed this big amazing world. I liked looking at the sprawling land and the houses and all those other cars! There's so much to look at. But when it was time to leave, the sky had grown dark and there was little to see on the turnpike (I don't like that word, and neither does DS.) What else could I do but settle down in the back seat and take a nap. Plus, I was exhausted. So much so, the next day I kind of took it easy.

DS and DJ were going to take the trip anyway, and rather than leave me home and have a dog walker stop by, they took me with them and I have to say, I prefer that option. I know DJ does, too. Since he's been furloughed (this week's big word!) from work, I think he's been my shadow. Kind of ironic. DS kind of agrees.

The road trip was successful and bodes well for future ones. Where else in the world can I go? We have family in lots of places. Maybe I'll get to Syracuse this fall, and then there are the 2.0 Keenes who have those twins I like to play with. They host Christmas (I think that's the holiday where there's a tree in the house—sounds silly, but DS says it's very sparkly.) That's still a few months away.

For now, I'm going to relax in my home. I'm gonna bounce and pounce and snounce, like I do. But when it comes time to sleep, I'm going to dream of all that is possible out there in the world. Staring out the window only gets you so far. I like the car. I'll always be the passenger. I may have long legs, sure, but I don't think I could find the accelerator. Also, just know, I would brake for animals.

May the road you travel take you on the kind of adventures I have, and beyond. Travel is fun. But boy, when you get home, not only do you have to unpack, you need to unwind. Time for a nap....

Thanks for reading. See you next week. It's 7 days away. (That's a hint on my next theme.)

Love, Shadow Baby

"Hey. Bruce Wayne Menter here. I am a 10-pound Pomeranian, but don't let my size fool you. I am a fierce human protector, named after Batman. But as soon as I know you, I'll snuggle you all day. This is the pawfect book to explore the life of my furry friend, Shadow. I give it a 10/10—hey, just like my weight! I'd recommend this for a tail-wagging good time."

Bruce, Pomeranian, Ft. Lauderdale, FL

Diary Thirty-Seven A - Special Edition

Hi Everyone, it's Shadow. This will be a quick one, a bonus entry.

Well I've had the best year, and I've celebrated lots of things. Today I got to wag my tail in celebration of DJ on his birthday.

I love our walks and our snouncing and our playtime. I know he feels the same (even if it's before 7 am!). Along with DS, we have the best time. DS gave DJ a gift tonight—a book of photos featuring me and so many friends and family. But mostly just me.

Yeah, the years progress but that means we take greater appreciation of all we have. We have love and health and happiness. We have each other.

I'm a happy dog. I love that I make DJ happy.

See you all Sunday for the official entry, Volume 38.

Love, Shadow Baby

Diary Thirty-Eight

Hi Everyone, it's Shadow. Most weeks I talk about new words I've learned. But this week, it's all about...numbers! (Not something that computes well with DJ or DS.)

Here's what is going on. Just as DS celebrates his birthday in the 6th month, DJ has a birthday in this 9th month, and it happened just 2 days ago. Did you know that 55 years on this Earth equals 28,908,000 minutes? Gosh! Try multiplying that in dog years! And yes, DJ had to help me use a calculator to figure that number out. It only took a fraction of a second.

Another interesting number is 13. See, DJ was born on the 13th day of September, and this year that day fell on (DS is gasping!) a Friday. I've heard about this thing called a superstition (this week's big word, I can still get one in despite our theme) and apparently, people get spooked when the 13th falls on a Friday. It's supposed to incur bad luck. But if DJ was born on the 13th then that number is all right in my book (diary?)! 13 brought me good luck!

So, let's talk about this birthday weekend. On Saturday the 14th (which happens to be Aunt Peggy's birthday—that explains their close bond!), we had friends come over. 13 in all! 14 if you count me, and why wouldn't you? Wow, I had fun playing with all of them. 3 of us went on a walk. DJ looked so happy. They had 4 pizzas and 50 meatballs and 1 cake. I had my usual meal. DJ also got 2 tickets from DS to see his

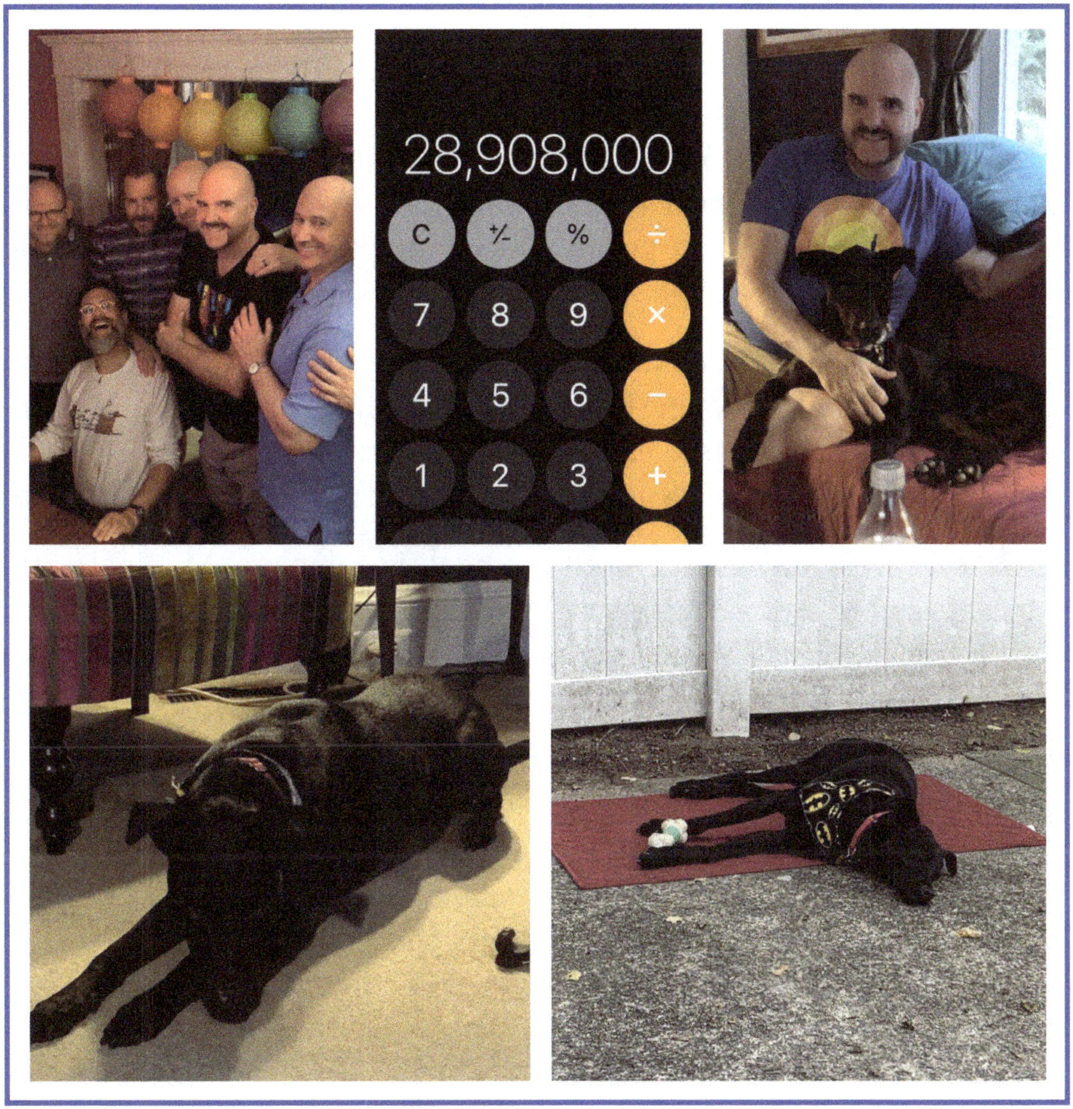

favorite band. The concert is next Tuesday, 2 days away. So, I'll be home alone for a bit that night. I'll get 1 dog walker stopping by.

Lastly, I want to talk about another birthday. One of DJ's favorite authors, a nice English lady named Agatha Christie. Today, the 15th of September, she would have celebrated her 129th birthday! Wow, she and DJ born just 2 days apart, and both like to write mysteries. DJ says one of her books inspired his desire to be a writer. Also, his love of trains. In all, she wrote 66 novels and 14 short story collections. That adds up to 80 books!

DJ (DA?) has written 42 books (and counting), with so many in the writing or development stage. Me, I'm hoping for just this 1 book to get published. It's currently on submission to 3 publishers. Keep your 4 paws crossed and wish me luck for a deal! DJ is acting as my agent. DS gets to write the introduction! I'm 100% into this!

There are 14 weeks remaining until my book is complete. My final entry will be Volume 52, and it's gonna be a doozy! (DJ made me write that word, slang from 18th century England. I bet Dame Agatha used it!) See, even though I wrote all these words today, I'm still focused on numbers. Want proof? There's only 10,080 minutes remaining until I post entry 39.

While all this adds up to a full life, it's better summed up by subtraction. 3time minus 2 Daddies minus 1 Shadow equals 0 Complaints.

By the way, all the numbers I used in this entry add up to 28,918,888! As always, thank you for counting...uh, reading.

Love, Shadow Baby

Diary Thirty-Nine

Hi Everyone, it's Shadow. This week I give you a time capsule I call A Day in The Life of a Dog. It's more exciting than you would think!

But first, a bit of context. See, it's been an interesting month so far. DS is back to work teaching the kids about art, this week something called Pariscrafting. Sounds messy! As for DJ, he suddenly went back to theatre. His schedule is...different.

What's with the 10 pm shows? Boy, does he get home late. So, for them, chaos reigns.

As for me, I like to keep life simpler. I stick to a routine. Let me explain....

7:00 am. I stir, stretch my long legs. I need to, because they've been curled up all night long. Usually DJ gets up with me and lets me out into the yard. I kind of just breathe the air, realizing it's a new day, one filled with the unknown. Then it's breakfast time! Ooh, I love it. A mix of dry kibbles and saucy chunks of meat, I devour it. Next up is my walk. I crazily pounce around the house until DJ relents and we leash-up. Afterwards comes a big drink of water from my bowl in the yard,

followed by a game of Triple Fetch!

10:00 am. Time for some reflection. DJ sits in the yard, reading a book for an hour. I join him, lounging on my red carpet and chewing on my nylabone or chasing my Bacon Ball. Sometimes a bird or a squirrel grabs my attention and I run back and forth and bark. But it's usually a nice, peaceful moment of the day. Just quality time with one of my Daddies.

12:00 pm. Alone time. DJ tends to leave for a couple hours to run errands or get some writing done. But that's okay, I like down time. Especially when it's accompanied with a Kong, stuffed with a treat and a schmear (that's a funny word!) of peanut butter. It's always an effort to get that treat out of the plastic toy. I guess my Daddies like to challenge me.

3:00 pm. That's when everything starts to change. Most days, DJ packs his bag and leaves for work. An hour later DS comes home. (When do they ever see each other!?) Me, I use the time to stare out the window, waiting for DS's car to pull up to our house.

5:00 pm. Dinner time! Yum, more of the dry kibbles and the rest of the can of the juicy wet food! And you know what? Then I get another walk. DS and I visit the neighborhood and say hi to the kids and dogs and neighbors. Sometimes DJ can be with us if he's not working. I wag my tail and do my business. Oh, I chase cats, too.

8:00 pm. Night grows quieter. I can either sleep on the living room sofa by myself, or I can chill out on the den couch with DS while he watches a scary movie. I wonder about DJ being so far away in the city. I know he's thinking of us, too.

12:00 am. Midnight. Life has calmed down. The blinds come down in the living room, mostly to stop me from barking at...well, whatever. Cats, people, trucks,

imaginary things. (More on that next week), I get a last treat and then it's time to settle and sleep. DJ likes when I join him, snouncing at his feet. And with that, I close my eyes and A Day in the Life of a Dog is complete.

What a joy it is when the sun rises and I get to do this all over again. Every morning is like a fresh chance at life. A renewal of the happiness you already feel. IF DJ and DS had tails, I know they'd be thwapping theirs just like mine! Embrace life. Morning is a reminder of all you have, and all that awaits.

Thanks, as always, for reading.

Love, Shadow Baby

Diary Forty

Hi Everyone, It's Shadow. This week I'm going to speak (so to speak) about The Art of the Bark.

First, I like that phrase. It's rhythmic. But it also gives voice to me, my reactions to the world, my way to say hi to everyone I meet. Humans speak words. That's how you communicate. Me, yup, my language is barking. Where we all come together, though, is in the eyes. We always know the intent behind the words...or bark.

DJ and DS don't always like when I bark. I'm kinda loud and energetic. But let me explain why. Because behind every bark is a thought, a reason.

Let's start with the neighborhood. So many folks have their lawns tended to. These lumbering trucks come down the street, trailers attached. Lawn mowers and such on them. They make a lot of noise, so I need to let them know that this is my block. I jump on the sofa and my paws claw at the windows as I remind them they're on my turf.

Other things make me bark. When I'm on my walk, there's of course the cats at the house down the street. I lunge at them and bark, but then there's the Pitbull on the corner (his name is Rambo!), who barks more aggressively than me. It kind of makes me whimper. But once we safely pass his yard, I'm myself again. For some reason, when we walk along the main road, I like to lunge at vans and cars. DJ halts the walk, holds my harness tight. But I still bark at those passing vehicles.

In the yard, the change of season has introduced a new element for me to focus on. In the sky, I hear all this squawking and it turns out, it's a gaggle of geese. (I like saying that.) They fly in packs, the cooler weather sending them away from the shore. I stare up into the blue and I leap and I (yup), bark. To them I'm just saying see you next summer.

Another thing that makes me bark is when DS and DJ have those phone-things in their hands. At night, when it's dark in the living room, the light from those devices distract me. I see reflections on the walls and ceiling, and it causes me to pounce and growl a little bit. A growl is a more sinister bark. DJ just calls me a tough guy, but I think he's being facetious (this week's big word!).

Lastly, I have a different kind of bark. It's quieter, with a melancholy (whatever that means!) mourn to it. I've written about the cute little white dog, Milo, before. I like seeing him and when he passes by the house, first I bark. I'm trying to get his attention to say hi. That's really all I'm ever doing when I bark. But after he goes home, I let out a lingering wail. It's my way of letting my Daddies know that I'm sweet and I have a soul and that I'm trying to communicate my feelings. Then they hug me and I feel better.

Suddenly the barking stops. I know I don't have to say anything more. I just embrace the embrace. Love doesn't always need words. Just a beating heart. But in this story is a good reminder to me: don't overreact. You might knock down the curtains. Oops, my bad.

Thanks for reading.

Love, Shadow Baby

Diary Forty-One

DJ Q&A Edition

Hi Everyone, it's Shadow. I'm gonna mix it up for the next two weeks and give my Daddies a chance to talk. DJ decided his should be done in a Q&A format. (DS might have his own idea for next week.) So, for now, let's get going. This should be fun.

S: Hi, Daddy. Thanks for doing this.

DJ: Thanks, Shadow. I'm happy to be here.

S: So, since this is my diary, let's keep things all about me.

DJ: Don't we always?

S: (My head tilts in confusion.) You're not funny.

DJ: But you are. That's what I love most about you.

S: This is my interview, let's not get ahead of ourselves. So, give me your first impression of me. I've heard that first impressions matter the most.

Like when you saw DS, you knew he was the one I think.

DJ: That applies to both of you, yes. When I saw you behind that plexiglass screen at the SPCA, our eyes locked. You lifted a paw and gently rubbed it against the screen. I knew right then your gentleness.

S: And then you two took me home. I remember that day, it was torrential (this week's big word) outside. So much wind and rain.

DJ: We did. Good memory. And we recognized right away that first weekend, your sweetness.

S: Yup, that's me I love a good snuggle.

DJ: You mean snounce.

S. That's a silly word. Now let's get back to the laughterness.

DJ: That's not a word. Remember, I'm a writer.

S: Um, the way I see it, we've got gentleness and sweetness, so why not laughterness? You make up words all the time. Come on, snounce?

DJ: Funny boy. Sometimes fiction becomes reality. Because I had a dream of once having the most perfect dog in the world. Look what's happened.

S: Aww, thanks, Daddy. I know I'm not perfect, not with that early morning wake-up and walk I pounce on about. But I come pretty darn close. Cute goes a long way. Okay, final question, if you could sum up our relationship in a quick paragraph, what would it say?

DJ: Gosh (as you would say), just when you think your heart can't grow any bigger, those closest to you do something to remind you that there are no limits to

the fullness of a heart. Every day with you and DS I feel the beat of your hearts, I feel your love. I smile all day, even when I'm away at work. I embrace my sweet boys and know my world is perfect.

But what makes my laugherness most of all? When DS and I share a hug at the end of the night and you come trotting over and you leap up and join us in your nuzzly, nippy way. In the end, you know that this house is blessed with three hopeful souls, all looking—and finding—happiness, one smother hug at a time.

S: Happiness. That sounds nice. See, Daddy, I told you all those kinda good words end in "ness." I'm sticking with laughterness. And by the way, that was two paragraphs. Come on, can we go play Triple Fetch now? (We did, see the photo!)

Thanks, as always, for reading.

Love, Shadow Baby

"I, like Shadow, am a rescue. My two Dads take such good care of me and read me *The Shadow Diaries*. I love the adventures that Shadow shares, and I'm hoping that one day we will share a play date. I need a new friend and he seems ideal."

--Charlie, West Highland White Terrier, Matawan, NJ

Diary Forty-Two

DS Q&A Edition

Hi Everyone, it's Shadow. Last week I got to interview DJ and it went so well. So, this week, it's DS's turn. Let's see what he's got to say!

S: Hi Daddy. Ready for my questions?

DS: Shadow, if I've learned anything about you, I'm ready for anything.

S: Ok, first question. I have so many names. DJ likes to call me Shadow Baby. But you have a more formal name, which I like.

DS: Oh, you mean Mr. Shadow. You can be so goofy at times, Shadow, but other times you're aloof. It reminds me that you're your own animal. When you pounce around the house, I call you crazy. But when I'm watching a movie in the den, sometimes you're so peaceful in the living room. It's when the movie is over and we cuddle is when I think of you as Mr. Shadow.

S: Yeah, I like our nights. That's when DJ is mostly gone.

DS: He's got a weird work schedule. You and I, we stick a little closer to home. But then there's times when it's all three of us, and that's the best of all. Don't you agree?

S: Well, yeah, I do. But remember, I'm asking the questions.

DS: Noted.

S: What's your favorite thing you and I do together?

DS: When we're on the living room sofa. I take hold of you and bring you into my arms. I love the way you slide against me, almost making us one. You put your head back and nuzzle my neck. Your Chow tongue slips out and you give me a kiss. It's always a special moment.

S: I know sometimes I get rambunctious. Usually late at night when DJ comes home. You tell me I Need to Calm Down, like I'm a Taylor Swift (whoever she is) song. I just need to get the energy out of my system (or I need to do some late-night business in the yard) so I can sleep all night. You like that, right?

DS: I love that you sleep through the night. During the day, you play with your Bacon Ball and all your other toys, which we keep stored in a box in the den. Usually by the end of the day half of those toys are strewn about the house.

S: Strewn sounds like a fake word. I'll ask DJ about it. But yeah, I do like to exhaust myself during the day, but that's because at night I just want to be quiet with you. Snuggling up next to you, the lights down low. Just you and me. Both enjoying our time.

DS: You said snuggle. I think the word is snounce.

S: Oh, here we go again with that word!

DS: Hahaha!

S: Ok, Daddy, final question. If you can sum up our relationship, just like DJ did last week, what have you got to say?

DS: How much I love you. How much brightness you have added to our lives. From your early morning pounce to your evening walk. I think back a couple weeks ago. It was all three of us on a night walk, and when we came back to the house, our neighbors were outside. You played so nice with the little kids. Then a young family came by and said hello. Then another neighbor came by and she brought over Milo. It was like an impromptu block party, with you as the happy, jumpy, affable ambassador. You radiate such warmth.

S: Gosh, Daddy, that was so nice. (Wait, DJ told me to write, "that was so eloquent.") I don't know about DJ and his words. Yours were perfect. So, anyway, thanks for the chat, Daddy. Let's get some sleep, it's getting late. (And we did, see the photo!)

Love, Shadow Baby

"Mama Kris read me Shadow's stories all year—I want to go play with him and DJ and DS, too! Shadow got lucky like me and my brother and sister (who wouldn't sit still for the stories). You'll love each diary and maybe you'll go look for a furry companion like us."

--Jingle, Alaskan Husky, Blue Heeler/Dachshund mix

Diary Forty-Three

Hi Everyone, it's Shadow. Wow, the weather sure has changed. The yard furniture is in hibernation. And I'm feeling a bit lyrical about the seasons that fill our year.

Since I came to live with my two Daddies ten months ago, I've experienced the ever-changing world around me. I arrived here in Winter, I bounced around in Spring, I sunned myself in Summer, and now I'm having a breezy Fall playing with the leaves (see photo!)

Seasons are funny things. There are time shifts and there are changes in the rise and fall of the sun, and truth be told, my body feels them all. Let me explain.

Winter. I know it's coming (sounds like that would make a good tagline for a TV show). Flakes will fall, and if I remember from last year, our yard will be covered with a white blanket and crunchy ice. It makes playing Triple Fetch and running around a bit difficult. DS doesn't like it at all! But I had fun. My black coat kept me quite warm and it will again as the season approaches.

But then I think back to last Spring. The snow melted and the air grew sweet. I sniffed everything as I walked, almost like the ground was awakening from its cool slumber. Some days were cooler than others, but it didn't take the calendar too long to raise the temperature. The tree in our yard started to blossom, and you know what? So did I. I started waking up earlier than I had been before.

Once summer arrived...well, I woke even earlier and I'm not sure DJ liked that so much. See, the thing about the sunrise is that the earlier it starts its climb into the bright sky, the more happy I was to see what the world had in store for me. When I first came to live with my two Daddies, my daily walk happened around 10 am. By summer's arrival, it had transitioned to 7 am. I remember a recurring quote from DJ: "Shadow, it's too early."

Well, fall is here, which some people call autumn. Why do the other three seasons not have different names but this one does? There are fancier words to describe them all: equinox and solstice (whatever those mean). But what I've noticed about the arrival of fall is that it takes DJ much longer to get ready for our walk. Gone are the shorts and T-shirt. He's even had to wear a jacket lately! I get impatient waiting for him to tie his shoes. I pounce around with puppy energy!

I guess my point is that, as much as we treasure our routine, there are cycles to the weather, and in our environment, that affect our sleep patterns and our waking hours, our moods and motivations. We still do what we do, but we need to adjust to time, to temperature, to the rise and set of the sun. Snow will fall, flowers will bloom, the birds will squawk, leaves will fall. It's a year-round evolution, an ebb and flow of nature's beauty.

Each season will turn, turn, turn, but at the end of each day, we still reflect on our time and our life and realize all that surrounds us. Cold, warm, or breezily comfortable, the cycle of life inspires me daily to play with bouncy excitement. I hope everyone else feels the same way.

Thanks for reading. Next week...things are getting spooky.

Love, Shadow Baby

Diary Forty-Four

Hi Everyone, it's Shadow. Boo! It's a real Chiller Fest out there!

All month long, there's been this Omen of impending doom. Sometimes I feel like I want to hide, but not Six Feet Under. I'm no Psycho.

I think it's for The Birds to know that people are getting their Ghost on—DS is, beyond a Shadow of a Doubt, having fun watching his scary movies. Now I understand all the framed posters in the house. DJ looks at this holiday a bit more through a Rear Window, though I did witness him reading a scary book by some man name Stephen. He's supposed to be the King of horror. He writes long books!

Our Suspiria neighborhood....oh, I mean, our *suburban* neighborhood is littered with decorations. I Saw them all. On my walk, I get to sniff witches and bones and goblins and ghostly pirate ships. Even our own house has a doll in the tree (DS calls her Annabelle) and a witch on the door and four scary Pennywise's on the front pathway. Like everyone is sending up Burnt Offerings here, even in daylight! And Soon The Darkness will arrive and DS and DJ will carve Pumpkinhead and its sequel.

I guess I've just got to be a Maniac for this holiday. But I'm Conjuring next week already. Everyone is currently acting so strange, like they've gone all Stepford Wives for the month. Why do people want to Drink Your Blood, though in truth, I might be guilty of Eating My Flesh. (It's just an itch...I'm ok). All this spookiness is an

Alien concept to me.

Thinking about Halloween, I see there's gifts and lots of candy, so it's like Christmas but darker. You could almost call it a Black Christmas. I mean, right across the street, our neighbor built a makeshift semetery, for which I've had to put my paw down to say: no pets are allowed. But his young kids enjoy it. What do I say to that? Children Shouldn't Play With Dead Things.

I'd like to take a Shining to this day, but that might make me go all Cujo on my Daddies. IT wouldn't be right. One day is fine, but I'm not sure if I could Carrie on the tradition for all the Different Seasons. So, I'll just enjoy a good old Ghost Story and ride out the Nightmares and Dreamscapes until we get to The Other holidays. Yup, when it's all over, perhaps I'll hire The Exorcist to get life back to normal. The devil may be evil, but I also hear he wears Prada. (DJ made me write that part!)

Here's the thing about being scared. You can keep your Freddie's and Chucky's and Count Yorga's (now that's a Trilogy of Terror!), you can Scream all you want, but there's comfort in knowing on the next day we celebrate all the saints. That's The Thing! A new month arrives, a new Dawn (but not of the dead), more of a Midsommar. But until then, I'll grab a Chainsaw before any Alligator gets me. I'll Crawl away from any Massacre. (Sorry, Texas, I live in Jersey.)

Gosh, it's getting late, and my Jaws just did a big yawn. DS says Don't Be Afraid of the Dark, but tonight I'll sleep with the lights on. So, I'll end with this: no matter all the Terror surrounding us out there, I will do whatever I can to protect Rosemary's Baby.

Trick or treat! And thanks, as always, for screaming...uh, reading.

Love, Shadow Baby

Diary Forty-Five

Hi Everyone, it's Shadow. If I've learned anything this past year, it's that words matter. DJ lives by them. I guess we all do. It amazes me how many books and words exist and yet there are only 26 letters! So, I decided it would be fun to go through each of them, in order. Kind of a Shadow A-Z.

A is for Awesome. Because I am.

B is Bark. It's how I express my feelings.

C is for Cummings. It might be my last name.

D is for Dogs. That was an easy one. (Though I could have gone with Daddies!)

E is for Energy. Of which I have much.

F is for Funny. That would be me. (DJ's pretty funny, too.)

G is for Gosh. I use that word a lot in my diaries.

H is for Happy. Gosh, that one's kind of obvious.

I is for Independent. I like my alone moments.

J is for Joseph. The diaries are all his fault.

K is for Krazy. But I think that's misspelled.

L is for Love. It's what makes our snounces happen.

M is for May Street. My home. Thanks, DS.

N is for Nippy. Sometimes I get too excited.

O is for Orange. That's the color of my favorite toy, the Bacon Ball.

P is for Pounce. It's what I do.

Q is for Queer. Big deal. My Daddies are special.

R is for Running. Sometimes I race around the yard. It's fun.

S is for Shadow. I mean, Duh!

T is for Treats. I love them throughout the day!

U is for Upstairs. How I love to dash up and down those stairs.

V is for Very Cute. It's true. I am.

W is for Walk. My favorite!

X is for eXcellent. Ok, cheating a bit on that one.

Y is for Yes! Yes, I want a treat...a walk...to go out. To sleep...oh, speaking of...

Z is Zzz. At the end of the day, sleep awaits us all. (See photo)

Wow, so many words, so few letters! I'd say this diary entry was supercalifragilisticexpialidocious! How about that, so many letters in one word! I'm Poppins with excitement.

Thanks for R.E.A.D.I.N.G.

Love, Shadow Baby

"We had heard about *The Shadow Diaries* from our Mom, but then we got to meet Shadow in person (in dog?) at our house. He sure had fun running around our yard. How fun for us to be included in his first road trip diary. By the way, the Batman scarf? Woof? How about Oof!."

--Buster and Baxter, Cockapoos, Lansdale, PA

Diary Forty-Six

The Past Present Future Trilogy, Part One

Hi Everyone, it's Shadow. You know what happened this week? So much! I thought I was going on a road trip but what I went on instead was, well, a journey to the past.

I visited a magical place. A place that can be described with one word: Home.

Home, I discovered, isn't just where you live. It's a concept, the knowledge that you're welcome anywhere. There were many homes I visited this week and each of them was special, all filled with family and friends. But first we had to get there.

DS was supposed to take the wheel on Tuesday but he hurt his back. So, DJ drove, and wow, it was four and a half hours (that's even longer in doggie time). Truth be known, I'd never seen DJ drive before. But I hung out in the back seat. I looked out the window, as I do, but mostly I slept. I was a good boy. I kept hearing my Daddies talk numbers. 287. 80. 380. 81. 481. Like it was a scientific formula that ensured our arrival.

So, anyway, we arrived at a place DJ called The Track. That not what the sign said! This was where we were going to stay for two nights. Wow, a new home. I was a bit skittish on some of the surfaces but I got the hang of it. Mostly. But what's nice about The Track is that Grandma Rosemary lives there. Hey, that's her home! I got to see her apartment and hang out there. I met lots of people who also live in this community.

Another home I went to was Aunt Peggy's. That was fun. DS and DJ took Grandma out to dinner, so I stayed in East Syracuse. And guess what? AP has a big yard with lots of grass. The Greyhound (no, not the bus company) in me took to the yard immediately. I ran and I ran and ran some more. I slept well that night! I got to race around again the next day.

But then there were some quiet moments. Other homes, memories easily stirring within DJ. See, the village we visited is the where he grew up. Manlius, New York. (Which gives me now 3 states on my bucket list; CT I'm coming for you!) We drove to a few places, and each of them held meaning. DJ likes to write stories, but on this day, his stories were verbal. DS listened and as I do, I tilted my head out of curiosity.

We went to a place that's not quite a Home, but one that conjures the past. DJ brought us to a tree-lined, grassy area lined with, what he calls, memory markers. I got to sniff around and say hello to a man I would have called Grandpa. He lives elsewhere, high in the sky, which sounds

beautiful. I was told he was a Deacon (whatever that is), and as we arrived a song was playing in the car. Called "An Audience with the Pope." Someone was saying hi back.

We went for a fun walk along a pond, where there were lots of ducks and swans. I stared at them, bending my front paw. The Labrador in me was emerging. Those birds sure have a picturesque (this week's big word) home. Lastly, we walked up Smith Street to a house found at a crook in the road. It had a number on it. 114. That's where I learned DJ had lived here when he was a kid.

That's where Misty lived too. Their home.

Here's the background. On DJ's bureau he has a photo of himself at age 16 with Misty on the porch. On our visit, DJ recreated that photo--this time with me! DS took such a good picture. See both photos here. Do you see the resemblance, down to the red collar? And the rainbow shining in front of us? Another hello from the sky.

Our 3time trip was filled with so much love, so much family, memories of yesterday, all while making new ones to remember forever. Yeah, the car ride might have been long, but our journey backwards only took us forward. Yup, Home is more than a building. It's the sense of belonging.

Thanks for reading. I had a lot to share.

Love, Shadow Baby

Diary Forty-Seven

The Past Present Future Trilogy, Part Two

Hi everyone, it's Misty. During Shadow's recent visit, he reached over the rainbow bridge and asked if I could give him some perspective on life. Consider me the Ghost of Doggies Past.

First, a bit of background. Yes, my name is Misty. I was a Pittman. I came to be a part of the family when the now-named DJ was a boy. Just 8! For 14 years I lived in a dual-village named Fayetteville-Manlius. Which Shadow just visited last week. I led a happy life, even as I endured bouts of epilepsy. I didn't like those seizures.

Here's the nice part. When someone grows up with a dog, the world is somehow a brighter place. There's a different energy to your day. A sense of wonder and a lesson in compassion, wrapped up with one cute puppy. But it also comes with a dose of responsibility. I had lots of support around me. Dad, Mom, all my siblings. I know I was a dog but family is what I was.

Sometimes I would crawl under the coffee table, especially when there were fireworks. I wanted to be comfortable and safe. Other times I would sit companionably beside Dad's chair, usually after dinner. I knew my place! There were also times I would jump on the bed and I would cuddle with DJ. Ok, so I didn't always know my place. Mom did not like me on the furniture!

What I like to remember is what I awakened in DJ, a shy boy then. He learned a respect for animals. (Yeah, even cats. Mystic, I'm talking about you...) Dogs make life rewarding and fun and crazily impulsive. At times, sure you hear our bark but in a special way you also hear our quiet. What I know is that our voice conveys our moods.

Here's what I'm getting at. DJ's love of dogs began with me and grew over the years with dogs that other family members had. It's no surprise that Shadow resembles me, right down to the soft black coat and the red collar. And the sweet disposition. I'm so happy to have played my part in the bond between a one-time boy and his best friend.

Oh, speaking of best friend, the origins of Shadow isn't all about me. There's this guy, DS. I wish I'd met him (though my portrait hangs on his kitchen wall so I feel a connection). He had a sweet dog named Bongo—now that's a pouncy name. DJ fell in love with them both. Quickly. He and I and the others have fun running on a field that stretches toward the sun.

It's never easy when it's your time to cross that bridge. One Saturday morning, I wasn't feeling well. That epilepsy struck, and this one had a powerful impact. Mom and Dad called DJ, who was housesitting at Aunt Peggy's. He came over. They drove me to the doctor, who gave me something to settle me. I never came home. But my collar did, and my life's memories came with it. DJ still has that collar.

And now, because of this entire doggie history (although I was a her), Shadow has a beautiful life with two Daddies who love him and smother hug him and snounce with him. Gosh, the sentiments are just like I experienced but some of those words sure are different. They must have made more. If you've never had a dog, get one. The reward is tastier than a treat.

Thank you to Shadow for embodying mine and Bongo's loving legacy. A dog, as we all know, is just another way of spelling God. The bridge rises high in the sky, ensuring we're always watching over you. We are ever-present in your hearts and minds. Our impact is only made possible because of the family that rescues us. Remember is a word that doesn't forget.

Thanks for reading. And thanks again to Shadow for giving me voice in your diary. Maybe Bongo has a few things to say next week.

Love, Misty

P.S. This diary is dedicated to the memory of Ivy Lynn.

"My name is Cocoa, but my Mom, who loves chocolate, calls me Cocoa Bean. It's kinda like my cousin Shadow Baby! My parents picked me up from a farm in Pennsylvania and on the ride home told me all about our big family! One of the amazing things? That Shadow had written a book! Dogs can do amazing things. Home is love."

--Cocoa, Border Collie/Sheltie mix, East Syracuse, NY

Diary Forty-Eight

The Past Present Future Trilogy, Part Three

Hi everyone, it's Bongo. Even though I crossed the rainbow bridge a couple years ago, I'm never far away from home. Hearts can keep memories alive for a long time. Consider me the Ghost of Doggie Future.

My sister Misty had a few things to bark about last week and so, in the interest of equal time, I get my turn at Shadow's Diary. See, DS never knew Misty, but he sure has benefitted from the love of dogs she instilled in DJ. Let's be honest—it's what made My Daddies connect. I witnessed it!

I'll tell you my story, as much as I know it. I was hanging out at the SPCA somewhere in Jersey (to quote Shadow, wherever that is!). I was six years old, a big hound of a dog but ever so gentle. And quite cute. I waited for the right person to find me and take me home and gosh, did I get a good one! DS provided me a perfect home. I was a bit neurotic, so a calming influence was important to me.

See, DS had his own issues he'd gone through. Too much loss, too much sadness. He was looking for love and so was I, and so we found it together. What fun we had getting to know each other! I looked great wearing my bandana and rainbow collar. DS has style! It made me feel part of something—someone--special. A community of two. But we needed more.

Early on, I was scared. I was still getting used to the house on May Street. So, I did a crazy thing. I slipped out of the window upstairs and paced the roof of the back porch. The neighbors had to call Steve (and 911) because, well, it was sort of unsafe. Thank goodness everyone was looking out for me. That's when I knew I'd found my home.

But that's the point of being a dog. Humans love you and embrace you and snuggle you and make sure you are happy. We do the same. Life wasn't always fun though. I suffered from anxiety and so some days I would retreat to the basement to my crate. It sounds unpleasant but it wasn't. It was comforting. It kept me calm.

So, then something happened. This guy, I guess he's now called DJ, came to visit. DS met him first in that big city, but then he invited him to meet me. "I have a dog," DS is famed for quoting. DJ arrived and we met and he hugged me and he was so super sweet and I liked him a lot and so did DS.

Here's what happened. That first night DJ stayed, he wasn't feeling well. As DS slept, I took care of him. I curled up beside him, I offered comfort. I did what a dog does---and I didn't even know him yet. But I sensed a sweet soul within him, which Misty has confirmed. We bonded that night, and the next day, as DJ recovered, he realized there was more to this than a visit. The rest? it ended in I Do and Beyond.

Here's my message. Dogs are funny creatures. Sure, we love to eat. We love to sleep. But between the two, we know we have an obligation to those who adopted us. Who brought us into their family. We are there to heal, to make you laugh, all while you give us walks and, in my case, keep me off roofs!

DJ only got to know me for nine months. Time is an odd thing. It can stretch and feel endless. But a moment, that's another thing, it allows you to breathe, to stop and remember, to create new connections. And boy did we have our moments,

snuggling on the bed. DS would leave for school and suddenly I was home with this new guy. I knew the future had arrived.

When it was time for me to go, my two Daddies were with me. I felt their sadness, absorbed their tears That just meant I would always be remembered. Assured I had friends and family waiting for me, I knew I could enjoy the bright colors found on the other side. Knowing my portrait (painted by the same artist, thanks Uncle Don) hangs opposite Misty's confirms that I fulfilled my job. I was a dog.

Thanks for reading, and thanks to Shadow for letting me have my say in your inspiring diary. Time now for a restful nap.

Love, Bongo Boy

"With every keen observation, Shadow reminds us what it means to trust, then shares the love and wonder that makes a family. And, with great wisdom, teaches us the joys of being alive. His message is an inspiration we need right now, and I'm so glad my Dad, author Jay Quinn read this book to me."

--Henri, Weinheimer, Chapel Hill, NC

Diary Forty-Nine

Hi Everyone, it's Shadow. Oh. My. Dog, do I have news to report. There's a tree in my house!

Here's the crazy thing. Just hours after posting last week's diary, DS started assembling a tall green tree in the living room. He says it's artificial (that sounds like a big word), but still, I mean, it's a tree! Not outside, not one to pee on. It's inside. I mean, wow. What's going on?

First DS wrapped strings of colorful lights around the branches. The colors are hardly a surprise. DS is all about the rainbow! Meanwhile, DJ was unpacking boxes filled with shiny ornaments, glittery balls, and decorations of angels and reindeer. Their efforts took over my usual spot. I mean, they even had to move some of the furniture!

While all those ornaments—and there's a LOT of them—were placed on the tree, I paced and I ran and acted nervous but only because I was excited. That's when DJ explained it all to me: the holidays are here, the end of the year and all the wondrous celebrations that come with this time. I like that word: holidays. Sounds like fun because, well, it's a plural and that means there's more than one. Gosh, I had no idea what I was in store for.

I knew something was up when my Daddies came home and they had bags of food, more than usual. Then on Wednesday, 20 May started to smell of Turkey Day.

I heard DS call it Thanksgiving. But what I saw was a seasoned bird ready to go into the oven. I think my tail wagged non-stop as DS prepared it, the stuffing, the

potatoes. The rest of the cooking was done on Thursday. DJ started making vegetables. Yeah, not as excited about that.

Okay, but then there's more! It wasn't just about the food. We had company, and not just of the people kind. I had friends come visit too! I got to see that cute Maltese Ivory again and sniff her. And then a new entry into the picture, a beagle named Carter. I'd met his Mom Teena before and it was nice to see her, but oh, I had fun running around the yard with him. He's a little older than me so I kind of exhausted him. But I might have a boyfriend (see photo!).

It was nice to see Danielle and Todd too, and I liked how everyone made such an effort to be together. Seeing all our guests assembled around a table represented the spirit of the holiday. That turkey sure smelled great. It even tasted great (yup, DS gave me a small piece). They had pie and drinks of all types. I had water.

But ultimately it wasn't about what we all ate or drank, it was the laughter that filled our home, the photographs we took to remember special moments. Everything set amidst the glow of our tree. Color is life, it's what adds brightness to our days. The night ended but the sensibility didn't. See, that tree is not going anywhere anytime soon! Because as I mentioned, there's more holidays to come! I'll see more

people, more dogs, more bright lights, candles, celebrations. Sounds like I'll be the exhausted one!

Thanksgiving was great, but you know it only lasts for one day. This other holiday my Daddies call Christmas, it's not one day (or 12, as the songs says), it has its own season. There's falling snow and bright ribbons and bows and a jolly man named Santa, and underneath our trees are treats. Gifts conjured from the mind, but given from the heart.

For now, Happy Thanksgiving to all my diary readers. I hope your day was as wonderful as mine. It's you I'm so thankful for. Oh, and DS and DJ. Gosh, I can't do this without them. We'll have more holiday magic in the weeks to come. I keep hearing about this Rudolph guy. He's got a red nose. That's ok. Curious to meet him.

Love, Shadow Baby

"I haven't yet met Shadow but I sure do love to have his diaries read to me. My favorite entries are the sing-a-longs. They show off his cleverness and whimsy. He's a funny dog! It's good to laugh. Even though sometimes he made me cry. Ultimately, he made me bark! That's what we dogs do."

--Toffee, Lab Mix, Boston, MA

Diary Fifty

Special DS Edition!

Hi Everyone, this is Daddy Steve, making a Special Guest Appearance in this week's Shadow Diaries. I wanted to share with you an exceptional occurrence that recently transpired.

A few nights ago, Shadow and I were sitting on the living room couch. Both of us admiring the lights on the Christmas tree, while Vince Guaraldi played his piano on the Bose. It was night time, all was calm. My arm was wrapped around my furry Boy. He looked up at me and I peered into his amber eyes. I dissolved. A strange transference happened as I found myself suddenly plopped into the Land of the Greyadors! Talk about a place that was truly wondrous, and part of that wonder was what I DIDN'T find there.

In this Land:

There was no pained or anxious pondering about what could have been or what has yet to be done.

There were no children or teenagers worrying themselves sick, or feeling hopeless about being accepted for being themselves.

There was no money, and therefore no greed (except maybe some minor drama over the acquisition of Milkbones).

The only inappropriate touching was small nips at skirts or slacks to remind someone that "I'm cute and I'm excited to play ball!"

There was no deliberate cruelty or exploitation toward children or animals -- the vulnerable creatures.

There were no army tanks, AR-15s or weapons, because there were no wars, or other reasons to fight.

There was no pre-conceived notions or judgment.

Cages were only used temporarily, to keep animals safe and calm when their owners were away.

That sounds like a lot of missing components. Yet, within Shadow's amber eyes, in the heart of the Land of the Greyadors, there was so much that I DID see in this enchanted place:

I saw wide-eyed innocence that can only happen when one chooses to live constantly, within the moment.

I saw miles and miles of safe, warm, loving homes where Greyadors were fussed over and adored.

I saw trust and the expectation that all will be treated kindly and with respect.

I saw sensible safety parameters and rules in place to keep doggies safe from busy roads.

All smells were amplified big time - nearly 50 times (just like this volume number!) stronger than before, and it was used to assess everything with eagerness and excitement and wonder. Yummy food and meal times were anticipated and

appreciated with happy pouncing and elation.

Loyalty is expected and revered and cherished.

Quiet times with Daddies were deemed the best part of the day. Hugs, kisses, massaging furry legs, rubbing tummies, groans and sighs of contentment. Knowing that one is safe and loved. All of it unconditionally reflected through Shadow's wonderfully expressive and guileless amber eyes.

My time in the Land of the Greyadors felt too short. It all seemed like a brief tease, or a hint of an awesome flavor that you wanted another taste of. In the future, I know that there will be nights when I will be feeling blue, or discouraged about world events, even angry or exhausted or downright hopeless. I find comfort in the realization that when I need to be reminded of what truly matters, I need to look no further than to peer once again into Shadow's amber eyes. The Land of the Greyadors eagerly awaits a return visit.

Thanks, Shadow, for letting me have my say.

Love, Stevie Baby, aka DS

P.S. Uh, DJ cried over this. In a good way.

"Grab a chair and get comfy. This book is a real doggie treat!"

-Moxie, Manchester Terrier, Los Angeles, CA

Diary Fifty-A

Bonus Edition.

Hi Everyone, it's Shadow. First of all, thanks to DS for subbing for me yesterday. Love his heart, it's so big and giving. But I also had a few things to say (as did DJ), so as we come to the end of the diaries, I figured I'd share. Here it is.

Boy, has it been an interesting Autumn. We've had sun, we've had rain (including this morning) and so many leaves in the neighborhood! And this week....yup, we had snow. Um, I think that last part is called Winter. You're early.

But that's life, right? It's transitional and you need to adapt. Way back in August, DJ's show closed and he was gonna be a home a lot. Um, no. He got a new show and a different theatre in September and he'd been there ever since. Yesterday marked his last day there. He's so appreciative of everyone at the Booth Theatre for being so welcoming.

But it sure has been a challenging show. It might be short in running time, but when you have late shows on Saturday, Sunday, and Monday and you get home at 1:30 in the morning...gosh, it takes a toll. I try to delay my morning walk as much as possible but, hey, when you gotta go, you gotta go. Thanks, DJ.

DS has been busy too. Teaching, creating new art. He's had some time off but he's also had to deal with meetings and conferences and other events. This weekend

was important because five of his art pieces are being displayed at a gallery. I don't know what that means, but it sure sounds impressive. I am happy that DS is getting such recognition (this week's big word!)

As for me, I do my thing. I've had fun playing in the snow, sliding all over the yard. But I've kind of been in an introspective mood. See, it's been almost a year since my previous owners had to face the truth that I had to leave. I still don't understand the circumstances, which is why I'm unable to tell my new family about it. Thankfully I didn't stay long at that shelter. I mean, I knew someone would come adopt me. I'm just that cute.

And as you know, I hit the jackpot with my 2 Daddies. And, also, somehow I found my voice to be able to write these diaries. It's been so much fun telling my stories, living my life and pouncing around and making you all smile, taking a rest when done. You think a dog sleeps a lot? Yeah, but we're also thinking a lot and examining everything around us. We are curious creatures.

But I guess my point is that change is inevitable. It's a word with a specific meaning but there's an evolution to its execution. DJ's job changes (like tonight!), DS has two schools that each have their own schedule, the calendar shifts and we still keep doing our thing. Life is freestyle and it's love and it's supreme, and that's been the theme of this season. It's a show but it's life, too.

Wow, 50. It's an interesting number. To many, it's a halfway point. A time to look to your past and at what you've done, a time to look to your future to envision what hopes fill your heart. But for me, it's all about the present. Love what you do, love who you do, bounce and pounce in the moment because you never know when the moment is over. You know the sun still shines even when there are clouds covering it.

Thanks for reading (again). Next week...a Sing-Along!

Love, Shadow Baby

"Shadow is a lot bigger than me but that just means he's extra sweet. I have played with him at his home and I love reading his stories of life with this two Daddies. He has a special view of the world, seen through his beautiful amber eyes. Shadow is more than a friend, he's family."

---Ivory, Maltese, New York City

Diary Fifty-One

Hi Everyone, it's Shadow. This is a rare day. Both DJ and DS are off from work and they have promised a day of movies and specials and a yummy meal. It's just what they need! Just what I need too. I like seeing them together with me. 3time is important.

So in the spirit of the day, all about fun, I offer you one last Sing Along.

See, we've shared a lot of experiencers this past year, but one of our most fun times has been during our songs. We riffed (that's a funny word) on My Favorite Things and the Brady Bunch Theme. But this week, it's the ultimate. And perfectly timed for the holidays. Rudolph!

Let's do it!

"You know Milo and Rambo

And Rusty and Rocky

Sebastian and Chloe

And Wally and Bea

But do you recall, the most famous pooch of them all?

Shadow the dark-nosed doggie

Has a big and beating heart

And if you ever hugged him

You would swear you'd never part

All of the local doggies

Like to bark and jump and play

They always like when Shadow

Walks along his usual way

Come one chilly Jersey night

DS came to say

Shadow with your sweet cute self

Won't you watch Rudolph tonight

That was fun! What's the big deal about a red nose? I think he's cude....he's cude.

But ok, DJ says there are other specials. Who is this Santa guy and why is he coming to town? And that mean Burgermeister. What's wrong with toys? Jingle and Jangle, you're not fooling anyone with Vixen being dressed as a dog. I'm a dog, so I know. And socks over his antlers isn't gonna work. Gosh, it's enough to Rankin my Bass. (Please forgive DJ the awful pun!)

The holidays are here! Love the season, love the day, love all who share your life and know there's always tomorrow for dreams to come true. Next week, Volume 52. The final chapter of my book....

Love, Shadow Baby

Diary Fifty-Two

Hi Everyone, its Shadow. I hear that this time of year, lots of people reflect on the past. My final volume is the perfect time for me to do the same.

Where were the 3 of us last December? DS and DJ were getting ready for Christmas, wrapping gifts and anticipating a joyous wedding during the summer! They had each bought gifts they knew they would like, secretly teasing each other about what was to be unwrapped. But the universe had another gift in store for them. Me!

December 20th. That's when I found myself living behind a plexiglass screen, in a small space. Worse than a Manhattan studio (whatever that is!). I didn't enjoy my stay there. I barely ate. Call it the SPCA diet. Clock to December 28th. You know the story of when my 2 future Daddies first saw me. It's practically an urban myth now! My life affair began anew that day when I came home to 20 May.

I hear a lot about this coming Christmas holiday. What it celebrates and what it means, what it inspires. Joy, hope, love, remembrance and a big word: tradition. I start a new tradition this year. Instead of spending the holiday at the shelter, I get one with my Daddies and extended family. Gifts abound!

DS got a special present this year, so let me tell you about it. His new family has this tradition (there's that word again) giving ornaments with your name on it, spelled out in glittery letters. DS got his just a few day ago! Because he said I Do. Our

family added 7 new additions to this tradition. Wow, there's a lot of us!

Then something amazing happened. A package arrived in the mail, and inside it...I got my name ornament, too! I was barkless! I mean, just wow. Thank you to the memory of Teddy and Summer for including me in the legacy of family dogs. What a sweet letter you wrote to me. My ornament hangs on the tree along with DJ's and DS's. I'm gobsmacked! (That's' a funny word.)

We're going on another road trip. I've been told Christmas with the Keenes 2.0 is so much fun. Games with those adorable twins and movies with my cousins and running around the yard, good food and treats. I'll get to play with Lily again! She came to my home in July, where we wrastled around on the floor like best buds. Probably gonna happen again, this time on her turf.

I guess what I'm saying is that family is forever. Holidays represent a chance to celebrate all you have and all you wish for. I think I already had my wish granted. A new year, a new life, a new chapter in the life of a lucky dog. I watched as DJ hung his name ornament on the tree, a tradition begun. He's had his since he was a little kid. Wow. The years sure do push on. Just like this year.

And so, to all my dear readers, I thank you for visiting every week to see what I've had to say. The Shadow Diaries started as a fluke, just a way to say hi, and turned into something special. DJ provided me the words. DS the inspiration. Me? I was just my funny, quirky, irrepressible self. Bouncy and pouncy and trouncy and snouncy, embedded (that's a big word) with all sorts of cuteness. And at the end of each day, just being loving and cuddly.

Volume 52 (gosh, that's amazing to write) brings a close to an awesome year, a journey of love and devotion, of stories of today and yesterday, both informing tomorrow. Sometimes I was silly. Sometimes I had serious things on my mind.

Sometimes I took a break and had guest stars: thanks to Gustavo, to Kong, to Misty and Bongo, to DJ and DS and all the other kind voices who replied to my posts.

I hope I've made your hearts full and put a special smile on your life. I also hope I've provided laughs and songs along the way. Until we meet again, I wish you all a Merry Christmas and Happy Hanukah and Happy Holidays, and to all, as Tiny Tim said (whoever he is), a good night. It's been an amazing year.

And with that, simply, The Shadow Diaries come to an end.

Wait, press the pause button! DJ just told me that his books always have an Epilogue beyond the final chapter. A last twist in the tail...uh, I mean, tale. So, looks like before this wonderful year wraps up I'll return with the true finale of The Shadow Diaries: The Inspiring Year in the Life of a Rescue Dog. After that, let's make this a book!

Love, Shadow Baby.

Diary Fifty-Three: Epilogue

Hi Everyone, its Shadow. DJ says there's nothing more satisfying then turning the last page of a book you loved. You reflect on it and you still don't set it down. You look at the cover and page through it, reliving characters and stories. Such a sentiment got me thinking. My book is turning its last page, an entire year's worth. There's a song lyric that sums it all up.

"Five hundred twenty-five thousand six hundred minutes, how do you measure a year in the life?"

It's a good question and one I'd like to explore in this, the encore edition of The Shadow Diaries. I'm forever grateful to all of you for following along on this year-long journey. Life isn't something you rent. You own it. It's yours. And if you take the y out, it's ours. I'm posting this on Saturday instead of Sunday, because today is the one-year anniversary of finding my Daddies.

I've had the best year and I know I will continue to have another as the calendar turns. Writing this weekly diary has been such a joy (I know DJ has had fun helping me and DS loves the Sunday morning surprise of what I share on any given week). But if DJ has taught me anything about writing, it's that some stories need an ending. He told me Volume 52 would be the end of The Shadow Diaries, representing an entire year. But it's good to have the chance for the final wrap.

As much as this journey is ending, know that mine continues in other ways. As

Selections From
RENT
Original
Cast Broadway
Recording

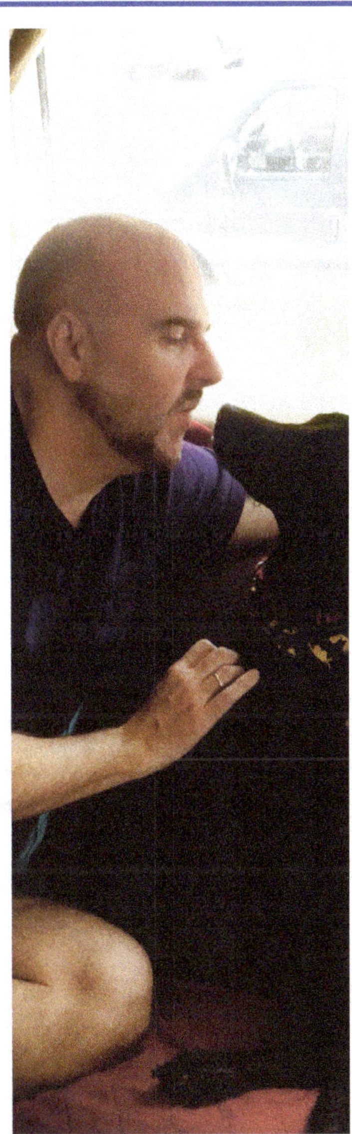

you know, I'm super happy in Keyport, and DS and DJ are the best parents ever. Sure, DJ may hug me too much (smother hug!) and DS loves to post FB pics and videos of me, but it's just the circle of life. Ultimately, I make my Daddies laugh and I enhance the bond between them and us. I know it's been a common theme in my diaries, but you must admit, it's a good theme and a reminder that smiles scare away the bad.

Humans and dogs, we're not that different. We eat, we sleep, we play, we pounce (ok, I do). But it goes beyond the basic needs. We dig deeper into the emotional component of what makes us us (can I use the same word twice?). We feel and we hurt and some mornings are so tired, but ultimately we endure. All of it happening as we explore this world in which we find ourselves living in. It's an adventure!

I've learned so much. DJ has told me about trains and a thing called Broadway, I've been educated in art and watched DS sit at the table and concentrate on a new painting. I've watched DJ pound away at the keyboard as he crafts a new book. Both of my Daddies embrace the creative spirit that turns our world beautiful, and you know what? I like to be creative, too. They've taught me that much. Because each day I try to mix up my routine.

I change the way I chase the ball. I change the way I take my walk. I bark and I wail and I play, sometimes with different results. I even change where I sleep each night. I guess I'm fickle. Sometimes I need my space. But before bedtime comes, what's always the same is the comfort I feel from my Daddies and the way we cuddle and, yes, snounce (the word of the year!) What it all boils down to is the pursuit of happiness. Maybe pursuit is the wrong word. Because I know I already found it.

It's time to concentrate on turning my weekly diaries into a published book. DJ submitted a video of me to this show he likes to watch each day, Good Morning

America. They responded and said they hope to use it. and will let us know. Wow, I could be on national TV! DJ's working on getting someone from that show to write an introduction to the book. They love stories of rescue dogs—like me. Though I no longer need rescuing. No guarantees, but if I know anything about my Daddies, they are persistent (a last big word!)

As the sun goes to sleep and the moon rises to its ghostly glow, I realize 52-plus weeks have passed. So many mornings and nights have gone on to history and all of them have been magical. Seasons of Love indeed. Knowing a New Year approaches in a few days, it's got me thinking back to that original question in that song lyric I quoted.

How do you measure a year in the life?

The answer? How about love.

Eternal Thanks, Shadow Baby

P.S. This one's dedicated to DS

"Reading *The Shadow Diaries* warms the heart and then suddenly you find yourself laughing. Or barking. What great fun for this Sly Guy to read every Sunday with Mom, Dad, and little Maddox. A book that's all about the love of family."

--Sly, Black Labrador/Beale mix, Albany, NY

"I live in the city, Shadow lives in the burbs. I walk on sidewalks. He gets to experience grass! We might lead different lives, but there's a universal theme in *The Shadow Diaries*, that it's all about being a member of the family. I always have fun playing with DJ when he visits me. Shadow sure is lucky to have two Dads. I wag my tail whenever I am read a new diary entry. You'll woof this down!"

--Bernadette, Cockapoo, New York City

About the Author(s)

Shadow is a now-three-year-old Black Labrador/Greyhound mix, with his amber eyes and his beautiful coat, he is insightful beyond even dog years. He is the pride of the neighborhood and easily makes friends with neighbors both two-legged and four-legged. He loves his walks, his treats, and his Daddies. He lives in New Jersey and promises he will post occasional future entries.

Joseph Pittman is the author of fourteen novels, including the acclaimed Linden Corners series: TILTING AT WINDMILLS, A CHRISTMAS WISH, A CHRISTMAS HOPE, THE MEMORY TREE, and CHASING WINDMILLS. Stand-alone novels include WHEN THE WORLD WAS SMALL, LEGEND'S END, BEYOND THE STORM, and the crime novels LONDON FROG, CALIFORNIA SCHEMING, TWO TODD TALES, TWO MORE TODD TALES, and the three-part serial thriller THE ORIGINAL CRIME.

Under the pseudonym Adam Carpenter, he is the author of the best-selling Jimmy McSwain Files: HIDDEN IDENTITY, CRIME WAVE, STAGE FRIGHT, GUARDIAN ANGEL, FOREVER HAUNT, FRESH KILL, and the forthcoming SECOND SHOT.

He lives in New Jersey with his husband, Steve, and, of course, Shadow.